MISTRESS OF FIRE

TALON COVENANT

MAR/10

Mistress Of Fire- Talon Covenant

First Edition

ISBN: 979-8-9994905-1-3 (Print)

979-8-9994905-0-6 (Ebook)

Cover Design: Markee Books
Interior Design and Layout: Markee Books
Published by: Richard P Marten

CONTENTS

CHAPTER 1

THE CEREMONY OF MAKING

Night devoured the poppy field. Shandar ran, each breath burning in her lungs, the weight of darkness pressing against her spine like a physical force. Ahead, a golden light pulsed between the distant trees, salvation, if she could reach it.

The light retreated as she advanced. Always the same distance away, no matter how she strained.

Behind her, laughter rippled through the darkness, low, patient, amused. The sound of a predator toying with its prey.

Shandar's foot caught. The ground rushed up to meet her, and she landed hard, palms and knees scraping against…

Not dirt. Not poppies.

Amber wheat stalks swayed around her, bathed in sudden, impossible sunlight. Her heart hammered against her ribs, the tranquility more terrifying than any darkness. This peaceful field didn't belong in her nightmare. Something was wrong.

Fire bloomed across her neck. She slapped at it, finding nothing.

A lone bird wheeled overhead against a brilliant blue sky. Its cry pierced the silence, a single note of warning.

"Soon," whispered the laughter, now at her ear.

Darkness flooded back like ink in water. Shandar scrambled upright, clawing at the air, trying to escape what she couldn't see. When she turned, the sound slammed into her skull. She clapped hands over her ears.

And saw it.

The dragon's face materialized from shadows, scales like blackened armor, eyes burning with ancient knowledge. It regarded her with the patient malice of a creature that had watched empires crumble.

"The Mistress will fail," it said, each word grating like stone against stone.

Shandar dropped to all fours, memory of her mother's stories flashing through her mind, dragons meant death, always death. She crawled over sharp rocks that bit into her palms. Ash filled her nostrils, the scent of destruction already accomplished.

The dragon's prophecy followed her: The Mistress will fail. Was she the Mistress? Would she fail?

Through tear-blurred vision, she spotted it, the source of the golden light. A medallion spinning slowly, suspended from a low branch at the forest's edge. Not retreating now. Waiting.

Shandar lunged to her feet and ran. The dragon's breath scorched the air behind her.

As she crossed the threshold into the trees, the chaos stilled. The light steadied, illuminating a path that led to a small stable nestled against rolling hills, her childhood home before everything changed. Dawn light bathed the weathered wood in amber hues, promising safety that had never truly existed.

Her fingers closed around the medallion. The metal was cool against her skin, then warmed, and vanished.

It reappeared, hanging from a leather cord around a man's neck. He stood before her, steel-blue eyes regarding her with a gentleness she hadn't expected, hadn't known to want. Something in her recognized him, though they'd never met. His presence called to something buried deep within her, something that had survived her mother's betrayal and her own broken childhood.

Before she could speak his name, a name she somehow knew, icy fingers clamped around her ankles. She looked down in horror as skeletal hands erupted from the forest floor.

"No!" she cried, reaching toward the man with desperate fingers.

The hands yanked her backward, out of the forest's protection. The man's face contorted in alarm, one hand outstretched toward her, too late.

Darkness swallowed her as dragon fire roared overhead, consuming everything in its path.

Shandar bolted upright in her cot, a half-scream dying in her throat. The darkness pressed against her skin like a living thing, but the nightmare burned brighter, dragon scales, skeletal hands, that medallion. She forced air into her lungs, one breath, then another.

Outside, morning sounds filtered through the warped window frame. Fishmongers shouting prices. Cart wheels on cobblestones. The salt-tang of sea air mingled with roasting meat from the street vendor's cart. Her stomach clenched with hunger, but she couldn't move yet. Not until the city's familiar rhythm drove back the dream's whisper: The Mistress will fail.

Shandar stretched her arms overhead, focusing on the wooden ceiling slats where shadows played in the early light. Reg returns today, she thought, allowing herself the smallest smile. That meant meat pies if she could manage to look happy for him. Sixteen now. Her season of Making had finally arrived.

"Soon," she whispered to herself, the word an echo from her nightmare that she reclaimed as her own. Soon she would lead her own life, away from this place. Away from Mother. Away from what had happened. The thought hardened within her like a stone. No one at the temple would ever know what Mother did.

Her home, a crumbling adobe hovel called Seer's Tears, huddled against the city wall beside War Gate. Fishwives and merchants mocked its grandiose name when they thought she couldn't hear. Shandar tied back her copper-red hair with a leather cord, letting the breeze cool her neck as she stared out at the harbor.

A floorboard creaked. Mother stood in the doorway, rocking on bare feet, her eyes too wide, too fixed. That familiar emptiness where sanity should live.

"He's coming." Mother's lips stretched into a smile that never reached her eyes. "I've seen it."

Shandar turned away. "Who?"

"The prince." Mother's voice lilted with childish excitement.

"Not Blair. Not this again." Shandar focused on the dream catcher hanging from the ceiling beam, the one spot in the room Mother's gaze always skipped over, as if it didn't exist. Shandar had woven it herself, hiding three drops of her blood in the center where the threads crossed.

"He's hiding as Luther, but it's him." Mother's fingers plucked at nothing in the air. "Just in time for your Making ceremony."

"I'm not princess material." Shandar swung her legs off the bed, planting her feet on the cool dirt floor. She stood, using her body to push Mother back toward the doorway. "Besides, you always said I'd marry Blair anyway."

Mother grabbed Shandar's wrist, her grip surprisingly strong. Her gnarled fingers dug into the skin. "I've seen it." Her voice dropped, suddenly lucid. "Six hundred fifty years of peace have left us vulnerable. No palace guards anymore. Just ceremonial fools in pretty uniforms." She leaned closer, her breath sour. "The time of change is here. The stars are shifting. You must be with Blair."

Something in Mother's eyes, a clarity that frightened Shandar more than the madness, made her shrink back, hands rising to shield her face. An old habit. A child's defense.

"After what you did to me," Shandar whispered, "why would he want me?"

Mother's face went slack, the moment of clarity vanishing like mist. Shandar slipped past her into the narrow street, where dawn painted the eastern sky blood-red.

Hours later, Shandar returned, stepping silently through the doorway. Mother lay curled on her pallet in the corner, finally asleep, her breathing shallow and quick like a frightened animal's.

Shandar gathered her meager possessions: a wool dress for winter, a linen cloak for rain, three copper coins hidden beneath a loose floorboard. She wouldn't need much at the temple. That's what Reg had promised when he'd offered to take her north with him.

Something glinted at Mother's feet, a small yellow-red god's eye woven from yarn and sticks. Shandar's throat tightened. They had made it together when she was seven, before the visions came, before Mother changed. Before that night when Mother had…

Shandar snatched up the god's eye and tucked it into her pocket, hating herself for wanting it, for still loving some ghost of the woman who had once been her mother.

Reg would be waiting by the harbor gate at noon. He was like the brother she never had, steady as the tides. He would take her to the temple where her new life waited, no princes, no prophecies, just the path she chose for herself.

But as she shouldered her small pack, doubt gnawed at her certainty. The dragon's warning echoed in her mind: The Mistress will fail. Was she running toward her destiny or away from it?

Dawn's cold light crept across the Temple of Lashnar's ancient walls as Shandar paused at the threshold. Her heart hammered against her ribs, each beat a reminder that this day would change everything. The gate towered before her, twice her height, its pale wood carved with hundreds of hands cupped toward a rising sun, both welcoming and warning.

She took a breath and stepped through.

Inside, Head Mother Sido Byers stood waiting, her earth-toned robes flowing like autumn leaves around her sturdy frame. Her brown eyes, calm as still water, assessed each sixteen-season-old who entered. When those eyes found Shandar, they lingered for just a heartbeat longer than necessary.

"Welcome to your Making," Sido said, her voice carrying to every corner without seeming to rise above a whisper.

Shandar hesitated before stepping into the courtyard. An ancient oak dominated the center, its gnarled branches reaching toward the lightening sky like supplicants. Around its massive trunk, sixty or so young ones gathered with their guardians. They lined the ivy-draped stone walls, their whispers and nervous laughter tangling in the morning air.

No one looked at her twice. No one's eyes widened in recognition. No pitying whispers followed in her wake. The anonymity was a balm she hadn't known she needed.

She squared her shoulders and clutched her small travel sack tighter. One night here, she promised herself, then my real life begins. Away from Mother's prophecies. Away from the shame of Seer's Tears.

The murmurs faded as Sido raised her weathered hands. The ceremony began with a chant that started low and swelled until it filled the courtyard:

"May the gods grant us vision..." The crowd's voices rose in unison.

"Make us whole!" The words resonated against the stone walls.

Silence fell like a heavy cloak. Sido stood motionless beside the oak, her eyes closed, her face turned skyward. The quiet stretched until it became uncomfortable, until Shandar felt the weight of it pressing against her chest.

Then something nudged at her mind, not a voice, but a pressure, urging her forward, pulling words from somewhere deep inside her.

Her feet moved before she willed them to. "I..." Her voice cracked, and she swallowed hard against the dryness in her throat. She tried again, louder this time, the words ringing clearer: "I am Shandar, daughter of the Seer of Tiereny. I seek my purpose." A pause, then words she hadn't planned: "Who will guide us?"

The hush that followed crushed against her like a physical force. Faces turned toward her, eyes widening, mouths parting in surprise. Her momentary courage withered. She took a half-step backward, wishing she could disappear into the ivy-covered walls.

Then Sido's head tilted at an unnatural angle. Her eyes rolled upward until only whites showed, glowing faintly in the dawn light. She raised her palms, and Shandar gasped. Symbols burned on the Head Mother's skin, a dragon writhing on her left palm, an oak tree spreading roots across her right.

The symbols pulsed once, twice, three times.

Sido clapped her hands together.

The sound cracked like thunder, and golden light erupted from her palms. It rippled outward in a shimmering wave, washing over each young one in turn. Shandar watched, transfixed, as the light approached her, beautiful and terrifying all at once.

When it touched her skin, her breath caught in her throat. Heat and cold battled within her chest. The courtyard, the oak, the faces, all blurred and faded. Memories flashed behind her eyes, her mother's unblinking stare, the dream catcher above her bed, the steel-blue eyes of the man from her nightmare.

Then the world went black.

Blair guided Blaze down the frost-bitten trail that snaked above Tiereny, each breath clouding before him like fleeting ghosts. Twelve seasons gone since he'd last walked these hills. Twelve seasons since he was seven, when the wild-eyed Seer had cradled a red-haired infant girl and proclaimed their marriage.

"How would the third son of the realm ever hope to be King?" His father's laughter had cut deeper than the winter wind that day.

Blair's hand drifted to the nearly empty coin pouch at his belt. He needed Rowan's promise of work to be real, not another tavern boast. The familiar weight of hunger had become his most loyal companion these past months.

By midday, Moor's Tavern would appear around the bend. One more job. One more expedition into the Waste. Then perhaps enough coin to silence the hollow ache in his belly, and the deeper one in his chest.

In the Temple courtyard, young initiates knelt before the ancient oak, faces solemn with anticipation. Sido moved among them like water, her weathered hands guiding each to touch the carved wooden gate that stood sentinel beside the tree.

When Shandar's turn came, her fingers trembled. The polished wood felt unnaturally warm against her palm, almost alive. She closed her eyes.

Darkness. Then…

A silver path unfolded before her, winding through mountains that scraped the sky with jagged teeth. Dark forests breathed around her, branches reaching like grasping hands. The path ended at a cathedral whose spires pierced the night beneath the glow of twin moons.

A sound tore through the vision, laughter that froze her blood and cracked the air itself. Behind her, something massive shifted. Heat washed over her neck. She turned.

A beast loomed, scales black as midnight but threaded with veins of brilliant turquoise. Wings unfurled like storm clouds. Eyes that held galaxies fixed upon her.

Shandar gasped, the connection severing like a cut thread. Her knees struck stone as she collapsed, the vision's fragments still burning behind her eyes.

As twilight painted Moor's Tavern in shades of amber and shadow, Blair nursed his last cup of watered ale, watching the door. One client. That's all he needed, someone willing to pay for his knowledge of the Waste, that barren hellscape where most men perished within days.

His fingers traced the worn grip of Comet, the sword he'd carried since his fourteenth naming day. The court's gilded halls seemed a lifetime away now. He missed the certainty of his place there, if not the suffocating weight of protocol. Out here, he answered to no one, a freedom that tasted sweeter than any palace wine, yet left him adrift.

A shadow detached itself from the gate's postern, an old man with hair like storm clouds and eyes as green as spring leaves.

"Where is my wife?" Blair called the old joke spilling from his lips before he could reconsider.

The stranger's response came soft as falling snow. "She departed for the Coven of Making not a full moon past."

Cold flooded Blair's veins. His hand found Comet's hilt, drawing the blade in one fluid motion. "How do you know me?"

The man's smile spread slowly, revealing teeth too sharp for comfort. "Everyone knows the third jewel of the crown carries the sword Comet."

Blair's mind raced through possibilities, assassin, spy, madman, but found no answer that didn't end with blood. After a heartbeat's hesitation, he sheathed his weapon with a nod that committed him to nothing and stepped toward the tavern door.

Behind him, a sound like crackling parchment made him turn.

The stranger's form rippled like heat above summer stones. His eyes narrowed to reptilian slits. Twin flames curled from his nostrils, illuminating scales that had been skin moments before. The creature, no longer remotely human, sank into the earth as though it were water, leaving only scorched grass and the echo of whispered words:

"Wait until you see what we build for you, young king."

Blair stood frozen, staring at the empty space where impossible had become real. Within the tavern, voices rose in drunken song. Beyond the village, darkness gathered like an army. And somewhere between, a third son with an empty purse and a legendary sword wondered which threat would claim him first.

Beneath the shadow of a distant mountain, wizard Gwydion stood before his creation, breath shallow with anticipation. The bronze colossus towered three paces tall in the forge's dancing light, its bull-necked frame promising destruction, metal hands crafted for a single purpose, to crush the Willow dynasty that had stolen everything from him.

Arcane veins pulsed beneath the stone floor, feeding the black altar at the chamber's center. Each throb sent tremors through Gwydion's boots, the magic hungry, impatient. His round face and wild, untamed eyebrows gave him the look of a kindly uncle, a disguise that had served him well in the years since his parents' public execution. Twenty years had passed, but he still saw their faces when he closed his eyes. Still heard his mother's final words as the Willow soldiers dragged him away: "Remember who you are."

He had remembered. Through his sale to the mountain smiths, through the beatings and burns, through the nights spent memorizing forbidden texts while others slept. Hatred had been his companion, his teacher, his only friend.

From within his robes, Gwydion withdrew two objects: a chalice rimmed with thirteen blood-red rubies and a knife of black iron, its edge thinner than a whisper. The chalice had belonged to his father, the only possession he'd managed to hide when they came. The knife he had forged himself, tempering the metal with his own blood.

"It is time," he whispered, his voice echoing in the chamber.

He pulled a rusted chain hanging from the wall. Stone ground against stone as a section of wall rotated, revealing an alcove where a girl no older than sixteen stood bound with silver wire. Blonde hair hung limply around her tear-streaked face. Her eyes, wide with terror, reflected the forge's flames.

"Please," she whispered. "My father has gold..."

Gwydion summoned the chalice to hover before her with a mere thought. The girl's pleas died as he approached, knife raised. He felt nothing as he drew the blade across her throat, no remorse, no pleasure, only purpose. Her blood, surprisingly hot against his fingers, cascaded into the waiting vessel. Before the last drop fell, he pressed his palm against her wound, sealing it with a whispered word of power. Not from mercy, but necessity. The spell required her to remain alive, at least until the final verse.

He turned to the bronze colossus, its hollow chest cavity open and waiting. Carefully, Gwydion began the blood-magic incantation, words older than the mountains themselves. Each syllable burned his tongue, tasting of metal and ash.

"Flesh of demon, heart of steel, Through sacrifice, I bid thee real."

The blood in the chalice began to bubble, then boil, though no heat touched the vessel.

"Hatred forged through years of pain, Rise now at my command to reign."

The liquid glowed with sickly light, illuminating the chamber's shadows with crimson radiance. The girl whimpered as the magic pulled at her life force, her skin growing ashen.

"Blood of innocent, freely taken, Power of vengeance, now awaken!"

With steady hands that belied his racing heart, Gwydion poured the glowing blood down the creature's throat. For a heartbeat, nothing happened.

Then energy erupted from the colossus with the force of a thunderclap. Gwydion was hurled backward, skull cracking against his workbench. The forged altar split down its center, ancient stone shrieking in protest. Darkness flooded the chamber, extinguishing every torch and candle, leaving only the creature's pulsing red glow as illumination.

Through watering eyes, Gwydion watched his creation transform. Bronze plates shifted and separated as scales formed beneath, iridescent black with edges sharp as razors. Muscle and sinew wove themselves between metal joints. Coarse hair sprouted along its spine, each strand writhing like a living thing.

The girl's final scream pierced the chamber as the last of her life force transferred to the beast. Her body crumpled, empty now, nothing more than discarded material.

With its first inhalation, the creature's massive chest expanded, shoulders straightening to their full, terrible height. The sound of its breathing, wet, heavy, hungry, filled the chamber. Candles rekindled themselves, flames burning blue, then white, illuminating the newborn horror.

Gwydion struggled to his feet, tasting blood where he'd bitten his tongue. Two crimson eyes, like molten iron fresh from the forge, studied him with unnerving intelligence. The beast took one lumbering step forward, then another, each footfall cracking the stone beneath. Gwydion's hand moved to a protective amulet at his throat, old fear warring with newfound power.

The creature halted before him, its shadow engulfing the wizard. It lowered its massive head until those burning eyes were level with Gwydion's own.

"Master," it rumbled, voice like stone grinding against stone, resonating in Gwydion's chest.

The word sent a surge of dark pleasure through him. He straightened, wiping blood from his lip, triumph replacing fear. This was the moment he had sacrificed everything for.

"Nudzh," he named it, the ancient word for vengeance in his mother's forgotten tongue. "The world shall tremble before you. We go to meet the Conqueror."

The beast inclined its head in acknowledgment, a terrible smile revealing teeth of jagged bronze.

And thus, the days of the Willow dynasty, seven centuries of rule, of prosperity, of arrogance, teetered on the brink of annihilation.

CHAPTER 2

VISIONS OF LASHNAR

Shandar jolted upright, every sinew taut. Sido's calm command still rang in her ears: "Meet your room-mates. Assemble at dusk." The soft edge in Sido's voice, like concern, haunted her even now.

She swung her legs over the edge of the simple bed and winced as the polished floor sent a cold shock through her feet. Five identical beds formed a row; each held a sleeping figure. Underfoot, wooden planks wove into shifting patterns charged faintly with the Temple's magic. No candle on any dresser flickered, though the windows yawned open. The whitewashed walls were bare, unyielding.

Through one pane she glimpsed the meditation glade, a single bench beneath twisted grapevines. Through the other lay the courtyard where she'd crossed into the Temple of Lashnar hours ago. That memory sent a ribbon of ice through her veins.

A groan broke the hush. One girl pressed trembling fingers to her temples. Another stuttered about strange disorientation. A third, tall and defiant, claimed no effect. Shandar slipped to the window overlooking the glade, back to them, voice low but steady: "This isn't ordinary magic. Lashnar's power saturates every stone here." She turned halfway. "Any lasting weakness?" She watched their faces. None but her seemed merely tired.

At the far end, a smaller figure huddled against the wall. Shandar strode across and crouched beside her, laying a hand on her knee. The girl's clasped hands didn't loosen. Fear or reverence, Shandar couldn't tell.

Movement outside caught her eye. Four novices pressed against the glass. Three young men strolled below with carefree laughter, swords at their hips. Behind her companion, Shandar felt the group lean in, hearts racing at a glimpse of normalcy.

She allowed herself a ghost of a smile before the footfalls returned. A thin elder in white robes stamped with Lashnar's silver emblem knocked once, then swung the door open. His pale gaze lingered on the trembling girl before he announced in a voice dry as autumn leaves: "Time for the Ceremony of Making. Follow me."

They filed down identical corridors until late-afternoon light spilled into a grove of lilac trees. A polished path wound toward a grassy amphitheater ringed with silent spectators. At its center, an oblong fire pit burned with unearthly steadiness. Behind it, a pole etched in shifting glyphs rose skyward.

Eleven robed figures sat cross-legged around the fire. Sido was among them, perfectly still in meditation. Shandar found her place at the far right of the initiates' line and braced herself.

A hush fell. Then the dancers rose in unison, weaving around the pit and tossing handfuls of shimmering powder into the flames. With each offering, columns of solid white light shot upward. A chant swelled:

LASHNAR, LASHNAR, HEAR OUR CALL!

MAKE THESE YOUNG SOULS WHOLE!

Shandar felt the words tremble onto her lips. The pole's glyphs flared orange in time with her racing heart. She closed her eyes, letting the ancient tide pull at her mind, until the world snapped silent, the white fire hanging heavy in the air.

A voice, deeper than human speech, rolled out from the flames:

"OH, MIGHTY LASHNAR, FATHER OF OUR FATHERS, GRANT THESE YOUNG SOULS THEIR VISION. BEGIN THE CYCLE. MAKE THEM WHOLE."

The ritual resumed, the fire pulsing white then orange. Visions barreled into Shandar's consciousness, burning through fear, leaving a crystalline calm in their wake.

Then came the scream. A sound she had only heard in nightmares. One of the novices collapsed, arms flailing. Sido stumbled as if struck, caught by another dancer before she could fall into the pit. Across the fire, Shandar saw a smaller figure rise with unnatural force. A second, more inhuman scream shredded the air. The pure white flames fractured into molten reds and yellows.

Shandar stood rooted, vision still half-lost in trance. Tiny flame-creatures skittered from the pit, their laughing sparks licking the ground. The dancers recoiled. Sido recovered and opened her mouth to shout, but a massive fist of living fire burst free and struck her, hurling her against the glyph-pole with bone-shaking force.

The smaller flame-creature darted back inside the pit. All but one. That last ember skittered toward the trembling girl Shandar had comforted. Before anyone could move, it dove into her open mouth. Her scream cut off mid-breath. With jerky, puppet-like motions she sprinted to the pit, shouted a single word, "GWYDION!", and hurled herself into the inferno. The flames soared in a pillar of white light, then settled back into a natural orange glow.

The amphitheater froze. The robed dancers blinked, releasing their visions. But Shandar remained statuesque, eyes rolled back in some lingering trance.

Hands shook her shoulder. "Wake up!" a frantic whisper hissed. But she did not move. Others rushed forward, alarm etched on every face, to carry her away.

Before dawn, Sido Byers awoke in her private chamber, the echo of that last scream burning behind her eyes. She probed the angry bruise on her side, every nerve alive with pain. In the corner, Landon lay slumped, knife still in his hand.

She touched his knee. "Landon." Her voice was low steel. "You need rest. In two hours, sound the horn. I want every acolyte, especially Shandar, in that hall."

He blinked awake, fear and questions in his gaze. "For what?"

"We're under attack," she said, voice sharp. "I don't know how far this reaches, but you will prepare every mind and blade within these walls."

Rain drummed on the dormitory roof as Landon arrived. Shandar sat on her bed, back rigid, eyes empty. Around her, novices whispered grief and dread. Landon's orders had already spread: the Head Mother would address them at first light.

In the vast dining hall, acolytes crowded the front rows, scholars huddled at the back, parents clutched children, guards stood rigid. When Sido entered, her gray robes plain, her bearing unbroken, a hush swallowed the room.

She met each terrified face. Then she spoke, voice honed by urgency: "Listen closely. Gwydion is no legend dormant in our texts, he is very real and he is here. He assaulted our sacred ritual and claimed one of our own. This darkness will not stop at this Temple."

Murmurs rippled through the hall. Sido's gaze sharpened. "We will not cower. In fifteen hundred seasons no soul has died during the Making, until now. We must steel ourselves."

She leaned on the long table, fists clenched. "At sunrise I leave to consult the ancient guardian. Riders will spread word to every city. We meet at the next full moon in the Place of Making. Until then, watch the skies, trust nothing, and prepare."

Without pause, she turned and strode out. Landon found her at the rain-streaked window, packing a travel satchel.

"Feed the novices. Enforce prayers, no exceptions, especially for Shandar," she ordered, dropping the bag onto the bed. Then she gripped his shoulders. "Pray for guidance… and for time. Someone else must know what we face."

He swallowed hard. "A girl died in our fire. What happens next?"

Sido closed her eyes, every year of her sixty-three pressed onto her chest. When she opened them, her resolve gleamed. "We will find out… and we will stand against it."

CHAPTER 3

SEEDS OF DISCONTENT

A spring breeze stirred the royal gardens, sending willow branches to kiss the still pond's surface. Moonlight transformed the water into a silver mirror. Rika Gresso knelt at its edge, her reflection fragmenting where ripples broke. One week as the queen's maid, and already failure's shadow dogged her. Disgrace here meant returning to her village with nothing but shame.

The pond stilled. Her reflection reformed: golden hair fastened with her father's silver filigree comb, evergreen eyes wide with doubt. A village girl among courtiers whose whispers cut like knives.

A second reflection materialized beside hers.

"Admiring the view?" The voice sliced the silence.

Rika spun around, pulse hammering. Prince Saad stood watching her, ash-blond hair falling across his brow, dark eyes set beneath copper-hued eyebrows. Court whispers named him the queen's unacknowledged son, gossip never spoken in polite company.

She dropped to her knees. "My prince."

"Rise." His hand brushed her shoulder. "Fresh faces at court are... exhilarating." He leaned closer, his breath warm against her neck. "Surely my attention honors you more than mere service?"

A chill ran through her despite the night's warmth. "I live to serve you, my prince. Command me." The words were proper, but beneath them ran iron.

His cheeks flushed. "A willing subject. Far more gratifying." He seized her shoulders and pulled her onto his lap. His mouth covered hers, insistent, demanding.

Rage exploded in her chest. She twisted free and struck him, the slap cracking across the garden. Silence fell.

Horror replaced anger. She had struck royalty. The law demanded her life.

Saad's hand flew to his reddened cheek, shock hardening to fury. "Come back here," he barked. "This instant."

Rika snatched her cloak and ran, tears blurring the moonlit path as she fled toward the palace.

King Vardon Willow pressed his palms against the cold stone sill of his tower study, watching his son climb the garden path, one hand pressed to his cheek. The king's chest tightened. Memory flashed, Ellis Whyte sweeping his legs from under him, her knee connecting with his temple when he'd presumed to touch her without permission.

"Ellis Whyte," Merric had said afterward, helping him up, "may I present Prince Vardon Willow, our next king. Told you not to touch her."

A soft cough pulled him back. Sholin A'Tai entered, his black wool cloak embroidered with a quarter moon and solitary star.

"Your Majesty," Sholin said, voice barely above a whisper. "Your son's improper attentions to new maids have continued two seasons now. Some refused him. This one struck back." He paused. "If witnessed, she must die."

"I will deal with that if it arises." Vardon's unspoken thought hung between them: She will not die. "Two seasons? I heard whispers but never connected them to Saad. How did I miss this?"

"That which is closest is often overlooked." Sholin moved to the desk. "He needs discipline. Send him with the Morag patrol at dawn. No rank, no privilege. The wasteland's harshness may teach him what words cannot."

Vardon's throat tightened at the thought of the frozen steppes beyond the Wall. But justice demanded action. "Very well."

A knock. Both men turned. Prince Saad entered, pale but defiant.

"You summoned me, Father?"

"Sire," Vardon corrected, his voice cold. "Sit." He paced the floor, boots striking the polished wood. "Your conduct disgusts me. You provoked her response. You're a prince, not a common brute. Do you understand the harm you do?"

Saad's knuckles whitened on the chair's armrests. He said nothing.

"At dawn you leave with the Morag patrol. Commander Andreas will know how to treat you."

Saad's face crumpled. "Sire, she is only a commoner."

"She, and all of her station, are why you wear that crown." Vardon's voice cut like steel. "Remember that in the ice and storms."

Saad rose and left without another word.

"He's bound for the docks," Sholin observed. "He hides something I cannot see. An astral scout might uncover it."

Vardon set down his goblet. The memory of Ellis's refusal burned in him. "I must see her," he said, and left before Sholin could respond.

Rika ran through empty corridors, lungs burning. Armored footsteps echoed behind her. She yanked open an unmarked door and slammed it shut, pressing her back against it until the footsteps passed.

She found herself in an antechamber. An arched entryway draped with blue silk lay ahead. Beyond it, someone's private quarters. Her stomach dropped. She'd escaped one danger only to trespass where discovery meant certain punishment.

She slipped through the silk hangings and froze at a gentle voice.

"Why child, you look terrified. What has happened?"

Queen Ellis sat on a lounge before a hearth, a leather-bound book in her lap. Her pale blue eyes pierced Rika with unnerving intensity.

Rika dropped to the floor, pressing her forehead to the carpet. "Your Majesty! Forgive me... I didn't... I never meant..."

Cool fingers touched her shoulder. "Rise, daughter. Nothing will happen to you here."

Rika lifted her head. The Queen of Monde was more striking up close than at court ceremonies. Ellis Whyte-Willow's oval face seemed carved from marble yet softened by concern. Her lilac divided skirt caught the firelight, golden embroidery shimmering along its edges.

With a jolt, Rika realized the queen knelt before her, their hands somehow intertwined.

"Your Majesty!" She scrambled to her feet. "Please, you mustn't..."

The queen's laugh was like wind chimes. "Hold, daughter. I don't move as easily as you. I've forty seasons on you at least." She rose with practiced grace. "Rika, isn't it? Come sit and tell me what troubles you. A face like yours shouldn't know tears."

They settled near the hearth. Only then did Rika notice the room, not the opulent chamber she'd imagined, but a space of refined comfort: light teak paneling, simple brass-fitted furniture, a bed draped with fine netting suspended from what appeared to be a living branch. The heart of the room was this sitting area: comfortable chairs, a lounge, and shelves of leather-bound books with gold lettering.

Rika felt the queen's evaluating gaze. She opened her mouth…

The mahogany doors burst open.

King Vardon entered, his face thunderous. Rika leapt up and dropped into a deep curtsy, arms spread wide, head bowed. Her body shook with renewed terror.

"So, you know what happened?" The king's voice was ice.

Rika kept her eyes on the floor, guilt clear in her posture.

"I know nothing," Queen Ellis said calmly, "except that this young woman came to my chamber so distraught she couldn't speak. Then you burst in like a stallion fleeing fire. Will someone please explain?"

The queen reclaimed her seat, gesturing for Rika to do the same. King Vardon took the vacant chair, his gaze never leaving Rika, who pressed herself against the chair back.

As the king related what had happened, Queen Ellis listened without comment, her face a careful mask. Rika twisted her hands in her skirt. Though Vardon appeared calm, his tapping foot betrayed his agitation.

When he finished, Ellis exhaled. "Where is Saad now?"

"Heading for the city, Sho believes."

"We'll address him later." The queen turned to Rika, her voice taking on a formal edge. "As for you... we cannot have someone who struck royalty among us. You must be dealt with."

Rika braced herself.

"We will send you as a king's emissary. In six or eight moons, this incident will be forgotten, and you may return to court."

Rika blinked. Exile instead of execution. "The penalty is death," she whispered without thinking.

The king's expression softened slightly. "That is the official rhetoric. I believe we can avoid mentioning this incident again. But you must leave, and soon."

Queen Ellis knelt before Rika, placing warm hands on her knees. Their eyes met, and Rika glimpsed something like maternal concern in the queen's gaze.

"Daughter," Ellis said softly, "go to your room and rest. Tomorrow someone will come for you. Follow their instructions as if they came from me." Her voice dropped lower. "We cannot speak again until after you leave. Remember: what you did was not wrong. Saad's actions were inexcusable."

The queen glanced at her husband. "Tell no one of this. Some would demand the old laws be enforced. The king and I have worked to modernize these statutes, but many resist change."

The warning was clear. Rika's fate hung by a thread.

"Tomorrow, you begin a glorious adventure." The queen cupped Rika's chin. "That is how you should see it, a glorious adventure."

Rika backed away with a curtsy, eyes fixed on the floor. As she left, one thought consumed her: I struck a prince. My life is ruined.

When the doors closed, Vardon and Ellis faced each other in silence.

"Tell me what you withheld from her," Ellis demanded, though uncertainty tinged her voice.

Vardon sat by the hearth and arranged kindling before lighting it. "Saad has assaulted three servants this season," he said quietly. "At dawn, he rides with the Morag patrol." He paused. "He dismisses them as mere commoners."

Ellis studied the brandy decanter, searching for comfort. She took the settee opposite him, shoulders heavy with unseen weight.

"They fear for the realm," Vardon said as flames caught. "History shows heirs sometimes must be removed for the crown's stability. If Saad ever claimed the throne..."

Ellis closed her eyes. His meaning was clear: Saad would be permanently removed from succession. Guilt stung her for never seeing her son's cruelty, even as she acknowledged he didn't belong here.

"You must deal with Saad," she whispered, voice unsteady. "I will handle Rika, and I will bring Blair home to prepare him for rule."

Vardon added another log, his movements deliberate. "Blair?"

"If Glorin falls, Blair must be ready." Ellis's fingertips tapped restlessly. "Rika will find him and escort him here."

As Ellis's silent tapping continued, shadows danced across the walls, omens of sacrifice and the unending price of the crown.

CHAPTER 4

THE QUEENS ERRAND

Rika's room felt swallowed by charcoal shadows, dust motes drifting like ash in the stale air. Golden sparks flickered behind her eyelids, reluctant to let her wake. She buried her cheek into the rough wool of her pillow, then forced her crusted lashes apart, wincing as grit scraped her lids. At the edge of the gloom, a tall figure stood backlit by a single candle, its melting wax forming orange rivulets down the sides.

"Rise. Day's slipping away." His voice was cool and relentless, like water wearing down stone.

She blinked twice, the last vestiges of sleep melting from her vision. He stepped aside, and the candlelight revealed every detail: skin taut over high cheekbones, a single braid of glossy black hair looping over one shoulder, a long coat of dark-dyed leather patched at the elbows. He wasn't old, but the angles of his face and the calluses at his throat spoke of wilderness more than courtly salons. A grin curved his lips, exposing teeth unnaturally white, disturbingly sharp. Then those coal-black eyes caught hers, and her pulse thundered in her ears.

"Get up. The Queen sent me to guide you." He flung a rough bundle onto her rumpled mattress. "Inside: buckskin breeches, a shirt laced with rawhide, sturdy boots. Dress and come to the hall. We leave at once." He pivoted on his heel and shut the door with a decisive click.

As the guard's footsteps receded, memories struck her like a hail of arrows: the Queens's chamber fragrant with lilacs and violets, King Vardon slamming his jeweled staff against marble columns as lightning flashed through stained-glass windows, Prince Saad's rough grip on her wrist, the crack of her palm across his cheek and the electric sting that followed. They were exiling her to save her life.

Her fingers trembled as she undid the coarse twine around the bundle. She lifted the stiff breeches, smelling faintly of tannery, then the matching shirt woven tight for travel. Beneath lay boots of supple lambskin, soles thick with stitching. She drew them on, each buckle a small battle. Before she'd straightened the final strap, the door banged open.

"What's so slow?" His voice rang sharper than a blade's edge. He stood framed in the doorway; damp light outlined his lean shoulders. "The Queen's orders are mine too."

"I...." Her heart thundered as she straightened, cheeks hot.

"Wear these." He tossed the garments at her, new jerkin, snug leggings, a dark cloak. "Modesty is a luxury. This is only the first change." He stormed off, leaving her breathless in his wake.

Tears stung her eyes, but she dressed without pause. In the dim corridor she noted with a shock: he and she now wore identical outfits, buckskin dyed black, cloaks clasped at one shoulder, and both their braids lay on the same side. She parted her lips to question him; a rough hand clamped over her mouth, nails grazing her skin.

"No questions until rest. Mirror my steps." He dropped his hand, voice lowered to a soft growl. "Understand?"

She nodded, swallowing. He slung a canvas satchel over one shoulder and moved ahead with a panther's grace. She followed him through the great dining hall where long tables sat cold and empty, past a row of kitchens where cooks murmured over steaming cauldrons and the scent of roasting meat clung to the air. He slipped into a narrow, torchlit passage she'd never seen before.

At last a heavy oaken door groaned open to the cool night. He locked it behind them, the key's metal kiss echoing, then tucked it into his jerkin. They set off northward, skirting the outer wall where ivy and wild blackberry thickets pressed in. Rika stumbled over a deep rut, her boot heel caught, and she pitched onto damp earth, the ground sucking at her cloak.

He paused, turning to offer a gloved hand. His fingers closed around hers, cold and strong, hauling her upright. Without a word he resumed his silent stride into the dark hush of pines and oaks. Each time she faltered, his silhouette loomed at the edge of torchlight, his head tilting as if listening for her breath, then he melted ahead again like a shadow.

Her lungs burned, each step a reminder that she'd never run like this before. Branches clawed at her cloak and cheeks, unseen creatures rustled in underbrush, and the world narrowed to the sound of her ragged breathing and the crunch of leaves underfoot. An hour or more passed, time slipped into one endless ache, until finally they broke into a clearing bathed in pale moonlight.

A ring of blackened standing stones rose from the grass, and rough seats hewn from tree stumps formed a circle around them. The tracker retrieved an earthenware jug from a hollow trunk, lifted it to his lips, and drained half at a pull that rose his sleeves around muscular forearms. Then he motioned her down. Rika sank onto one of the stumps, pressing cool lichen into her ankles.

"We have far to go," he said at last, voice soft like gravel sliding downhill. He set the jug on a mossy root and fixed her with those burning eyes. "Start with this: who are you, really? Why would the Queen trust you to me while I search for someone else?" One hand hovered over his knee.

Rika squared her spine, feeling the weight in her chest. "I travel as the King's emissary," she said, voice trembling but firm, "and I expect the courtesy due my station." Her chin lifted, recalling the proud tilt her mother once wore.

In an instant his hand flashed, a knife's flat side pressed to her throat, and the cold steel sank into her pulse point. Blood roared in her ears.

"Wrong tone," he hissed, voice low and dangerous, as he slid the blade back into its sheath with a dull click. He took another pull from the jug, wiping his mouth on his sleeve. "El said, 'There's a girl in the inductee wing. Bring her along.' You were an afterthought." He set the jug before her. "Drink. You'll want it soon." He studied her face. "You seem innocent enough. The Queen's like a sister to me."

She forced herself to breathe, summoned what courage remained. "Sir, introduce yourself," she murmured, twisting the braid at her collarbone. "Perhaps then we'll understand each other."

For a heartbeat he recoiled, surprise flickering across his features, before his expression hardened. Rika pressed on. "I am Rika Gresso, the Queen's maid. And you, master tracker, where are we headed?"

His whole form snapped forward; he gripped her arms with iron strength, yanking her to her feet so that the world tilted. His face loomed, every muscle taut beneath weathered skin; she whimpered, tears brimming. Then his grip slackened, the fire in his gaze cooling.

"I'll tell you this," he said quietly, voice almost gentle. "We've been sent to bring back Prince Blair."

Rika's heart lurched and stilled.

"You truly are just a maid," he muttered, stepping back into the moonlight. "I thought you were a noble's ward." He frowned, as if puzzled by her presence here. "Why send a maid south of the Divisor?"

Color drained from her cheeks and her legs gave way. She sank to the ground again, the night air whipping tears from her eyes as she realized the truth: exile, disgrace, the Queen's mercy all gone. Sobs broke free, echoing among the silent stones, and she wept for everything she'd lost.

Blair shouldered open the heavy door of Moor's tavern. Sunset spilled across the threshold, stretching his shadow into the smoke-hazed room. Two hooded figures in the corner tensed, hands drifting to hidden weapons. He dropped two coppers on the bar.

"Ale."

The bartender, a mountain of a man with a face carved from granite, slid a tankard toward him without speaking. Blair leaned against the scarred wood, eyes half-lidded but missing nothing. The central fire pit had burned low, casting more smoke than light. Farmers hunched over tables, mud still caking their boots, speaking in low voices about failed crops and rising taxes. A serving girl moved among them, her eyes vacant as if her mind had found safer refuge elsewhere. Near the back wall, two men whispered together, glancing toward the door every few heartbeats.

Blair caught the bartender's eye. "Know Finrod?"

The man's expression darkened. Blair's hand twitched toward his knife before he stilled it.

"Thanks." He carried his ale to a table near the dying fire.

He'd taken one sip when the door opened again. A thin man entered, a crystal pendant catching firelight before disappearing beneath his doublet. The newcomer paused, acknowledged the hooded pair with a nod, then approached Blair.

"Are you Luthor?" His accent shaped the words precisely, like a stonemason's chisel.

Blair looked up. "Finrod?"

"A pleasure." The man smiled thinly. "Join us. My friends would value your company." He reached for Blair's arm.

Blair moved faster than thought, twisting the man's wrist until pain hissed between his teeth. Finrod massaged his arm when released, amusement rather than anger in his eyes.

"No force needed," he said, settling opposite Blair. "We seek passage across the Great Waste to the Dragon Rest mountains."

Blair's heart hammered against his ribs. The Waste. Nine moons of needle-grass that cut like knives, of water holes guarded by things with too many teeth, of nights when the stars themselves seemed hostile.

"My fee will make the royal tax collector weep," he said.

Finrod produced a leather pouch that landed on the table with the unmistakable clink of gold. "Half now. Half upon reaching the mountains. We seek a stone."

"A stone?" Blair leaned forward. "Must be precious indeed."

"Beyond price." Finrod's slender fingers hovered over the pouch. "A thousand gold kings now. The rest when we arrive."

Blair nodded, mind racing with calculations. No stone was worth such payment. Which meant Finrod was lying, or the true prize was something else entirely.

"We leave at first light," Finrod said, rising. "Sleep well, guide."

Three days later, Merric led Rika through the crowded common room of the Wayfarer's Rest. Conversation stuttered to silence as they entered, then resumed with renewed vigor as the patrons decided two more travelers weren't worth their interest.

Rika followed him up a narrow staircase that creaked beneath their weight. At the landing, Merric unlocked a door with a brass key. The room beyond was small but clean, a bed with quilted blankets, a worn leather couch, and in the corner, a private washing area with a porcelain basin.

Merric inspected every inch: under the bed, the window latch, between floorboards. Only when satisfied did he turn to her.

"The bath will be ready soon. Use it, we won't find such luxury again for many days." He tapped the door. "Lock this when I leave. Open for no one."

A soft knock interrupted them. Two young men entered with steaming buckets, poured them into the waiting tub, and left without a word. Merric slid the bolt home and turned to leave.

"Is it safe here?" Rika hated how her voice trembled, betraying the fear she'd fought to hide for days.

Merric paused. For the first time, something softened in his expression. He knelt, bringing his face level with hers.

"Nothing will harm you while I'm here," he said, the gruffness momentarily absent from his voice. "Many would ransom a queen's maid, or worse. Rest. Bathe. I'll bring food and secure our next passage."

After he left, Rika waited until his footsteps faded before stripping away days of grime and fear. The hot water embraced her, steam rising to loosen the knots in her shoulders. She closed her eyes, allowing herself this moment of peace.

When she emerged, toweling her hair dry, she found the room transformed. A small table held a steaming bowl of stew, fresh bread, and a cup of watered wine.

And Merric, seated in the corner, watching her with those unfathomable eyes, as if he'd never left at all.

CHAPTER 5

MORAG PATROL

Andreas Vanderslyke, Captain of the Guard, crouched on the frost-slick ramparts, watching. Below, thirty mounted soldiers shifted in the dawn light, metal rasped, leather creaked, horses stamped. Their breath hung white in the bitter air. In the center waited Prince Saad, alone beside his gray gelding. Two stable boys gripped the reins, avoiding the prince's eyes.

Andreas exhaled. "A royal patrol? More like punishment."

The measured footfalls of the royal family echoed across Hero's Walk. King Vardon's sable cloak swept the stones; Queen Ellis's skirts whispered frost; Prince Saad's jaw clenched in forced deference. Andreas descended to meet them, armor heavy on his shoulders.

"Glorin was to meet us," the king said, his words clouding. "Have you seen him?"

"No, my liege." Andreas kept his voice neutral. "Shall I send for him?"

Vardon glanced at the rising sun, then dismissed the question with a gauntleted hand. The patrol shifted behind Andreas, a collective sigh, the clink of bridles, horses snorting plumes of white.

The first golden light spilled over the wall. Andreas approached again, catching the sour scent of fear from Saad as the prince gripped his gelding's bridle, the same beast he'd ordered gelded in a rage five seasons past.

"My lord," Andreas said, bowing until his breastplate scraped stone, "Blackrock lies two days east. To reach it by nightfall tomorrow…"

"Very well." Vardon's displeasure tightened his lips, but he nodded. "Glorin will catch up."

Relief rippled through the men. Saad bent to kiss his mother's cheek; a single tear caught the light on her lash. He extended a trembling hand to his father before mounting.

The great gate swung wide. As the patrol began to file out, a voice cut through the morning air: "Be alert!"

Andreas looked up. Prince Glorin's flaxen braid vanished behind the parapet. The king and queen froze, their faces suddenly bloodless. Without a word, they retreated into the shadows of the keep. Only Saad rode forward, into the rising sun.

Andreas remained in the churned courtyard, dust settling around his boots, a cold knot tightening in his gut. What transgression had earned Glorin's warning? And what fate awaited them beyond the walls?

A full lunar cycle later, Blair led three cloaked figures up Talon Pass. Wind screamed through the rocks, tearing at their seal-hide scarves. Hooves crunched on frozen scree. Blair halted beneath a towering black spur, the "dragon's talon", then vanished.

Moments passed before his face reappeared, pale against the darkness. "The rock hides a passage," he called. "The horses know the way."

One by one, the animals ducked through an invisible seam. Heat struck them like a furnace blast as they entered a perfect circular chamber. Three black sconces cast wild shadows across walls polished by inhuman hands.

Finrod pushed back his hood, frost glittering in his hair. "Ancient work," he said, stamping life back into his feet.

"Titan-made?" Blair asked.

"A curious shelter," Finrod replied. "But where's this talisman dealer?"

Blair approached one flame and thrust his arm directly into it. The fire curled around his flesh without burning as he found and twisted a hidden lever. A loud click echoed, and a curved section of wall ground aside, revealing a spiraling staircase.

They descended into polished onyx, an echoing hall lined with obsidian pillars, its floor split by a crimson carpet. Above, a prism chandelier scattered fragments of light. At the far end loomed massive doors of shifting golden filigree. Blair lifted a lion-head knocker and let it fall.

Thunder rolled through the silence. The doors creaked open.

Beyond stretched a narrow torch-lit corridor carved from raw stone. Blair stepped forward. "Tartus," he called, voice steady. "It's me, the rambling mouse, with visitors."

A bookcase pivoted, revealing a being that stole Blair's breath, broad-shouldered and golden-furred, with four powerful arms each holding a massive tome. Hooved legs clicked against stone as the creature stepped forward, gray eyes holding ancient wisdom.

"Tartus," Blair said, hand falling to the sword at his hip, "it's Mouse Willow."

Recognition kindled in the creature's eyes. It closed its books and settled into a striped chair that dwarfed it. "Young Willow," it rumbled, "how fares your father? He demanded news of the Magik unleashed upon the land. You arrived remarkably swift after the calamity."

Blair's throat tightened. "What calamity?"

"First, your purpose," Tartus said, waving a massive claw toward Blair's companions. "And these, elven sorcerers in disguise. Remove your Magik."

The three travelers exchanged glances. Finrod broke the silence, lowering his hood with deliberate slowness. He removed a crystal pendant from his neck. Golden light cascaded down his form.

Blair stepped back, breath catching. Where three ordinary men had stood, three impossible beings now towered, wheat-gold hair, skin with a verdant undertone, angular amber eyes, and ears that ended in delicate serrations. The scent of moss and loam filled the chamber.

"Impossible," Blair whispered, hand trembling as he reached toward them, then pulled back.

Finrod stepped forward with inhuman grace. "How did the king of Monde come to employ a Zoltar as his mage?"

Tartus inclined his massive head. "I serve Mertzanis's design, unbreakable loyalty to the realm and utter honesty. I guard these three volumes of the Trimort, for only they prevent spells from igniting."

Steaming platters appeared before them, rich stew, dark bread, glistening fruit. Between mouthfuls, Tartus recounted the Zoltars' betrayal of Icarius, the freezing of five ancients, and Mertzanis's creation of himself from the fifth soul.

Blair set down his spoon. "We seek a talisman and knowledge of the dark Magik. Are we in peril?"

Tartus's eyes narrowed as he spoke:

"Mistress of Fire, Seeker of Stone, Reflections in the eyes of Demons Unknown, Loins of Royalty, hold the Key. Only Triumph shall set the Nations free."

From beneath his chair, he produced a golden medallion. "Wear this openly."

Blair studied the medallion's face, crossed swords with different hilts, a red-gemmed eye on one side, a quarter moon and star on the other. Two depressions marked the back, one diamond-shaped, one circular.

The weight of it felt significant as he slipped it around his neck. When he released it against his chest, it seemed to vanish from his awareness.

"Where do I go to be seen?" Blair asked. "I cannot ride every street in the kingdom."

"The Temple of Lashnar," Tartus said, his voice suddenly uncertain. "At the next full moon. A general council gathers there."

Blair closed his fist around the medallion, cold metal warming against his palm. With Tartus's solemn nod, the four travelers slipped back through the passage, the prophecy hanging between them like an unspoken vow.

Three days earlier, in the Temple of Lashnar, Shandar Corpus hovered between worlds. A golden medallion spun through her vision, symbols blazing. As she reached for it, it leapt to a man's throat, steel-blue eyes burning into hers with something that felt like destiny.

"Blair," she whispered, jolting awake.

Cool hands steadied her. Novina, the apprentice healer, pressed a damp cloth to Shandar's forehead. "Lie back," she murmured. "You frightened us all." Her palms hovered over Shandar's limbs, sending ripples of gooseflesh across her skin.

"What did you call me?" Shandar asked, disoriented.

"Blair? No, not Blair." Novina's face brightened. "But you understood me! My healing rune worked!" She practically bounced with excitement. "Dalvan taught it to me. The Sages of Estridge will have to accept me now!"

"Cured me of what? A bad dream?"

Novina's smile faded. "Nightmares. Four days' worth." She tapped her foot impatiently. "We fed you, tended you. Tonight, my rune brought you back." Her voice dropped. Shandar closed her eyes, steadying her racing heart with her mother's Seer's mantra. "Fetch Sido for me."

"Head Mother Sido's gone, seeking the ancient guardian. Some say the Dark One claimed her." Crossed her arms and stared at Shandar.

"She left two days ago." Novina's jaw tightened. "And Irit died in the flames, taken by the wizard Gwydion. They're gathering to petition the king against him." She turned away, muttering, "I cured her..."

Alone, Shandar sank into meditation, sorting vision from nightmare. Poor Irit. The taste of ash and loss lingered.

A soft voice broke her concentration. "Shandar? Are you awake?"

Her heart leapt. Eyes still closed, she reached toward the voice, hoping for steel-blue eyes and a golden medallion. Instead, she sensed someone else, temple robes, a trainee's medallion. Green eyes, not blue.

Disappointment washed through her. She feigned sleep.

"I'm Thaylon," he said, knuckles white around a cloth bundle. "They assigned me to check on you."

She remained silent until he offered food. "No," she snapped. "Just go."

He bowed, hurt flashing across his face, and turned to leave.

At the door, she called softly, "Wait."

He paused, wary.

"Maderia, auburn hair, northern accent. Find her. Tell her I asked for her."

Relief straightened his posture. "At once, m'lady." He bowed properly and left.

Shandar exhaled slowly. She shouldn't have manipulated him, but Maderia would welcome the message. She whispered an apology to Lashnar as she drifted back toward sleep, the fragments of her vision, medallion, eyes, destiny, circling like hawks above her consciousness.

CHAPTER 6

REUNION AND REVELATION

Blair's frown deepened as he studied the silent elves riding beside Finrod. Yesterday they'd left the mountains behind, pushing hard toward the King's Road with the Temple only three days distant. He'd tried conversation, remarks about the weather, the terrain, but received only those strange whistles they exchanged between themselves.

"Why don't they speak?" Blair asked, his throat dry from the dust. "And what's with the whistling?"

Finrod shifted in his saddle, sunset glinting off his features, too perfect to be human despite the glamour. "Kumar rides left, Arbor right," he said, indicating each with a slight nod. "They're sworn to me until our quest ends. After years together, they've created their own language, whistles, hand signals, even the way they sit their mounts."

Blair shifted uncomfortably. "Are you truly the stone seeker Tartus spoke of?"

He couldn't help staring. Elves belonged in bedtime stories, not riding beside him on common roads. Their silence about the prophecy left him uneasy, wondering if they served some hidden purpose.

"I expected a simple guide," Finrod said, eyes dropping briefly. "Now I discover you're Prince Blair Willow. Everything changes."

Blair's fingers tightened on his reins. The crystal amulets that disguised the elves as human men were their only shield against unwanted attention. He drew a steadying breath.

"Our path is clear," he said with forced confidence. "First to the Mistress of Fire at the Temple, then east to Dragon Rest for your stone. The King's Road is fastest and keeps us from the Waste."

The words sounded certain. His heart was not. Was he following destiny or running from his royal obligations?

Finrod moved his horse closer, voice dropping to a murmur. "What drives King Vardon's son to pose as a common guide?"

The question hit like a blow. Blair recoiled, putting distance between them, yet something in Finrod's ancient eyes made the truth spill forth.

"At seven, I overheard my father say, 'The third jewel will never be king.'" Blair's voice hardened. "I mastered laws and letters, but stood invisible beside my brothers. Bitterness drove me to weapons training, but court jealousy relegated me to squire duties."

He paused as a merchant wagon rumbled past, then continued more quietly. "I trained in secret, tracking, hunting, surviving, then became the first Willow ever to slip away without permission."

His laugh held no humor. "I took the name Luthor, guided travelers, made my living. Found a child lost in the Waste and suddenly had a reputation. Now I'm told I must chase prophecy to Dragon Rest. I fled one predetermined life, why follow another?"

Finrod's eyes caught the firelight. "You chose this path, Blair. You could have refused my gold, never met Tartus, disappeared into the wilderness."

Blair's jaw tightened. "I spent your coin. My honor binds me."

"Your honor is what you decide it is," Finrod said. "Destiny may guide our first steps, but we choose what principles to uphold."

Blair turned away, heart pounding. A twig snapped; he whirled to find Finrod standing behind him, unnaturally still.

"Your choices thus far have shown wisdom," Finrod said softly. "But complete understanding eludes us all. Even after a hundred seasons, I grasp less of my own path than you do of yours." He gestured toward the fire. "Eat. We must move before full dark."

As Finrod stoked the embers and set water to boil, Blair stood frozen, those words echoing: a hundred seasons, and still uncertain.

Blair woke to the sound of hooves, his neck stiff from sleeping upright. His nightmare lingered, two faceless women pulling him toward a chasm with only a narrow bridge between.

He blinked at the dawn-lit camp. Finrod sat with Kumar and Arbor, but something was wrong. Arbor's skin gleamed green in the firelight, his features elongated and inhuman. Finrod caught Blair's stare.

"Fear not," he said calmly. "The crystals hide us from distant eyes. Arbor merely scouted in his true form."

As Blair watched, Arbor slipped a chain around his neck and shimmered back into human guise. Blair's pulse raced. Two secrets to guard now his royal blood and the elves' existence.

Finrod's eyes crinkled. "You spoke in your sleep battle cries, oaths, even women's names."

Kumar snickered behind his cup. Blair's face burned.

By midday they approached Riop. Farmers herded goats while merchants loaded carts. Blair stared at the activity with a hollow ache. "Six hundred fifty seasons of Willow rule," he muttered, "and our greatest legacy is watering stations."

They slowed at a caravan of Zingari wagons blazing with color, bound for Homestead's jubilee. Finrod eyed the bright cloth with suspicion.

"Pickpockets," Blair warned, though he secretly envied their freedom.

A barrel-chested merchant in orange and green hailed them. "Inspect our wares? A song perhaps?" Nearby, a woman in blue lace perched on a wagon seat, one leg swinging, her black hair tumbling over her shoulders. Blair straightened, suddenly conscious of his travel-worn appearance.

Finrod declined politely, they only had time to water their horses. Blair approached the merchant, his accent thickening. "Heard any news from Riop? Strange death at the Temple?"

The merchant, Logan Kuazar, leaned forward. "Trouble indeed. A wizard rose from sacred flames and snatched a virgin mid-trance. Some whisper he'll steal more children or raise the dead."

His daughter Kaleen's face paled. "Stay clear of the Temple. It's the most dangerous place now."

Blair nodded thanks, mounted, and urged his horse after the elves. He didn't look back, but her warning followed him, tangling with his dream's dark premonitions.

Night had fallen when they reached the Temple of Lashnar. The massive gates loomed before them, ancient runes carved into the stone glowing faintly in the torchlight. Their horses' hooves crunched on gravel, each step an affront to Kaleen's warnings about unseen watchers.

By the gate, a hunched figure huddled beside a meager fire, steam rising from a wooden bowl. He regarded them with beady, suspicious eyes.

"Dismount," he grunted. "No rooms left. Stables full, use the picket lines behind the oak. No fighting, no drinking. Magik enforces the rules."

Blair slid from his saddle. "We're bound for the fair," he lied smoothly. "Seeking work, gathering news."

The man shrugged, jabbed a gnarled finger toward stakes beyond the wall, and returned to his broth.

Inside the grounds, shielded lanterns cast uneasy shadows. Dozens of pilgrims huddled around small fires, their faces masks of fear unlike ordinary travel-weariness.

A toddler broke free from his parents and tottered toward their horses. Blair scooped him up before he reached the skittish animals, returning him to his embarrassed parents, who whispered their thanks.

Rather than join the main encampment, Blair and the elves built their own fire. Finrod studied the anxious pilgrims.

"Their faith is shattered," he observed quietly.

Blair nodded. "Never in recorded history has the Making ceremony been interrupted. They believed Lashnar's protection absolute."

Finrod placed a hand on Blair's shoulder. "Your people need a leader who cares."

Blair looked skyward, throat tight with unspoken limitations. His position in the succession left little hope of making a difference.

"This journey may be your true purpose," Finrod said. "Tartus's prophecy holds more than we yet understand."

When Finrod suggested they find the Mistress of Fire by revealing Blair's identity to the temple elders, Blair's shoulders tensed.

"Is there no other way?" he asked, hands clenched.

"It will be fastest," Finrod replied simply.

Finding no alternative, Blair stood and strapped his sword across his back.

"This is Comet," he said, drawing the blade. Firelight danced along its curved edge. "It's been in my family for six hundred fifty seasons, carried only by royalty." He offered the hilt to Finrod. "I earned it by besting my father in combat when I was eleven a tale that's followed me ever since."

The blade's balance was perfect, the leather grip worn by generations of Willow hands. From hilt to mid-blade, the word "comet" was engraved in flowing script. Blair sheathed it with practiced grace.

"This will prove my identity," he said. "In a kingdom this vast, few would recognize my face."

Finrod's eyes reflected the flickering flames. "You must tell me that tale of besting your father. It sounds... remarkable."

Blair turned toward the Temple, steeling himself for what lay ahead. The pilgrims' fires dotted the darkness behind him, small defiant stars against the gathering night.

CHAPTER 7

THE ANCIENT GUARDIAN

The log split with a sharp crack. Sido's head snapped up, heart hammering against her ribs. A shadow moved in the cabin's dim light. She exhaled. Only Landon, pressing a damp rag to Kaine's brow.

She eased herself from the rocker by the hearth, every muscle protesting. Two days without sleep had carved hollows beneath her eyes. The fire hissed at the fresh bark she'd added, sparks spiraling toward the blackened ceiling. Across the room, a pot bubbled over low coals, filling the air with rosemary and chamomile. Wind rattled the curtains, bringing pine scent to mingle with burning wood.

The cabin held only what necessity demanded: her chair, Kaine's narrow pallet, and a bookshelf burdened with ancient tomes and dust-coated vials. Herbs hung from the rafters – mug wort, juniper, nightshade, their scents releasing with each draft.

Sido's shoulders sagged. They had tracked this refuge for a day and half through mire and thicket. Convincing Kaine to help them had cost her more than the journey. The man was a husk now, skin like yellowed parchment stretched over bone. Yet he alone had seen Lashnar's true form, his sanity the price of that forbidden sight.

"Kaine," she said softly.

His chest rose sharply; fingers clutched at threadbare sheets. His clouded eyes found her. "Can I... serve?" The words crumbled from his lips.

She knelt beside him, ignoring the protest of her knees, and took his hand. "You must cross the planes," she said, "and learn who murdered the girl during the ritual." She forced her mind to Irit's final moments – hair aflame, eyes wide – willing the image into Kaine's sight.

His lips stretched into a vacant smile. "Is it my birthday? You brought cake?"

Pity burned in Sido's chest. She swallowed hard and whispered again, "Who killed her? Find out."

Something changed in his eyes. His breathing slowed. She rose, rubbing her neck where tension had knotted the muscles.

Dawn light filtered through the smoky window. Hours passed in silence. Occasionally, Kaine's lips moved, forming fragments: "iron wings... black blade... crimson sky."

Landon slumped against the rocker. Sido touched his shoulder. "Rest," she said. His eyes closed; the cloth slipped from his fingers.

She fed kindling to the embers. Cold dread coiled in her stomach as the air thickened, seeming to draw in upon itself. Her fingers whitened around the mantel until her pulse steadied.

"Not yet," she murmured.

A groan broke the silence. She turned to see Kaine sitting upright, movements unnaturally fluid. His head snapped toward her. Where eyes had been, two black voids gaped. His jaw stretched wide, and from his throat erupted a roar that shook the walls. Fire poured into the room, not in tongues but ribbons, slicing through air and wood alike.

Sido dove aside. Kaine's skeletal body contorted as flame consumed him from within. His jaw snapped shut, then opened to release a single word: "Temoc."

Landon lurched to his feet, face twisted in horror. Sido grabbed the iron dipper and flung broth at the burning figure. The liquid hissed into steam, but the flames only paused before surging higher. This was no natural fire but something ancient and hungry, devouring flesh and spirit together.

Kaine's form collapsed inward, reduced to ash that drifted down like gray snow. The word – Temoc – reverberated in Sido's mind, a name from forbidden texts.

Her legs folded beneath her. Darkness claimed her vision.

Cold water splashed her face. Sido blinked up at Landon's ashen features. Behind him, the bed lay empty except for a fine coating of silvery dust.

"He's gone," she whispered.

Landon nodded, grief hollowing his eyes.

She tried to stand but couldn't. Every part of her felt drained, each breath an effort.

"Temoc," she said into the silence. "We must warn the king."

Dawn light crept across Shandar's chamber floor, chasing shadows into corners. She woke with a start, fragments of nightmares about Irit's death dissolving as she opened her eyes. Her mind felt strangely clear, despite the dreams.

She settled into lotus position on her bed and began to chant. The familiar rhythm steadied her, but today something pulled at her awareness, beckoning her deeper than she'd ever gone before.

As her meditation deepened, colors exploded behind her closed lids, not seen but experienced. She tasted light, sweet and sharp on her tongue. The music of stars filled her ears. Heat gathered in her palms, and when she looked down within her mind's eye, crimson flames danced across her skin without burning.

From within this kaleidoscope world, a figure approached. A medallion gleamed on his chest, light pouring from him in waves so bright she had to look away…

"Shandar!"

Sido's voice cut through her trance. Shandar felt a strange weightlessness, then realized she was hovering above her bed, legs still crossed. Red flame wrapped around her body, radiating cold instead of heat. Within the fire, dark veins pulsed like ink in water.

Sido stood frozen at the threshold, her face a mask of wonder and fear.

The flames receded. Shandar blinked, suddenly aware of the attention. "What?" she asked, brushing hair from her face.

Sido approached slowly. "You manifested your essence as living flame," she said quietly. "You are a mage."

"A mage?" Shandar repeated.

"Yes." Sido's expression grew serious. "Next time, let me guide you. The power you've awakened requires discipline."

Something fierce and bright unfurled in Shandar's chest. "I'll try."

Later, under Sido's guidance, Shandar visualized her surroundings on a mental slate. She painted the chamber in her mind, capturing every detail from the stone walls to Sido's watchful expression. But when she tried to open her physical eyes while maintaining the vision, pain knifed through her skull. She cried out, collapsing.

Sido caught her, explaining gently that bridging spiritual and physical sight required practice. Despite the pain,

Sido couldn't hide her growing hope. A fire-weaver had emerged at last, perhaps in time to face what was coming.

Dusk fell over the King's woods. Birds fell silent as if holding their breath. A clearing shimmered with unnatural light that coalesced into massive scaled form. The dragon's presence bent reality around it, ancient and terrible. Its eyes burned like molten gold, seeing both present and future.

Two figures emerged from the shadows, Nudzh, tall and implacable, and behind him, Gwydion, barely containing his anticipation.

Nudzh knelt. The dragon's breath came as white flame, engulfing him completely yet leaving him unharmed. A massive claw lifted him by the throat.

"Rise," the dragon commanded, voice like stone grinding against stone. "No fealty is owed, only obedience in presence." A talon traced Nudzh's chest. "Name yourself."

"Nudzh," he answered, the word barely audible.

"Tormentor." The dragon's mouth curved in what might have been a smile. "Appropriate." It exhaled slowly. "The ritual succeeded?"

"Every step was followed," Gwydion confirmed, unable to hide his pride.

The dragon moved with impossible speed. One moment Gwydion stood grinning; the next, he lay in two pieces on the forest floor, surprise forever frozen on his face.

Nudzh didn't flinch. The dragon's eyes narrowed with approval.

"There is another you must face," it said. "A woman wielding fire. Do not underestimate her power." The dragon released him. "Command the horde. Bring down the Willows."

The air bent. Dragon and warrior vanished, reappearing beside a river overlooking the Wine Forest.

Above the water, a dark cloud hung unnaturally low, disgorging creatures into the world. They stood taller than men, horned and terrible, each bearing weapons that gleamed with cruel purpose. They gathered by the thousands, and still they came, an army born of nightmare.

Nudzh watched in silence, already planning the kingdom's fall. Nudzh leaned against a sturdy tree, its bark rough against his back. His bronze skin still radiated heat, faint tendrils of steam rising from his shoulders, a testament to the dragon's magic. His hands trembled slightly, the cool numbness of the dragon's voice echoing in his mind once more.

"Sweep east to west. I will join you at Tiereny. Here is what you need." A torrent of images flooded Nudzh's consciousness: detailed maps, fortifications, hidden passages, troop movements, each piece of information a crucial part of the plan. His lips curled into a cruel smile, his resolve steeled. He would not fail.

CHAPTER 8

THE KING'S BUSINESS

Before dawn, Sido moved through the silent east wing where the new initiates slept. At Shandar Corpus's bedside, she paused. This girl had summoned fire during her Making—raw, untamed power.

"Shandar," she whispered.

The girl's eyes flew open, wild with terror. An invisible force erupted from her, hurling Sido across the room. The Head Mother slammed against the stone wall, breath knocked from her lungs. On the bed, Shandar's blankets erupted in living flame.

"Breathe," Sido commanded, pressing her palm against the girl's shoulder despite the heat. "Control it."

The fire died instantly, leaving only charred linen and the acrid smell of smoke.

Shandar trembled. "Forgive me," she whispered. "I was dreaming of…" She stopped, unable to continue.

Later, Sido gathered the four surviving initiates in their chamber. She recited the prophecy in full, watching their faces grow pale in the candlelight.

"Seven chosen will face the darkness when it rises," she concluded. "The Mistress of Fire stands among you now."

Shandar clutched her pillow to her chest like a shield. "My mother said a prince would come for me," she confessed, voice barely audible. "Prince Blair. She said we would wed."

Sido's heart sank. The Seer of Tierney's daughter, the prophesied Mistress of Fire. Fate's cruel humor knew no bounds.

That afternoon, Prince Blair arrived with three silent escorts.

Sido closed the ancient tome she'd been studying. "Shandar awakened her power yesterday. She has no control. We need weeks, possibly months of training."

"Impossible," Blair said. "We leave at dawn."

Sido recognized the edge in his voice, not arrogance but fear. The young prince had seen something that haunted him.

"Show us this power," said the tallest escort, leaning forward with unnatural stillness.

The door opened behind them. Shandar entered wearing maroon leather armor that hugged her slender frame. Her red hair was pulled back, revealing the sharp angles of her face. Her green eyes found Blair's blue ones across the room.

Neither moved. Neither spoke. The air between them seemed to thicken, as if the prophecy itself held them in place.

"Your armor..." Sido finally said, breaking the silence.

"From my mother." Shandar's voice was soft but steady. "I found it this morning after you told me the prince had arrived."

The tall escort's eyes glittered with interest. "The Seer's daughter."

Blair took a step forward, his composure cracking. "You were foretold to me?"

Shandar nodded once. "I dream of your medallion." Her fingers twisted in her cloak. "Every night for months."

Blair's hand moved to his chest, drawing out a golden medallion from beneath his shirt. Shandar's breath caught.

"And I," Blair said quietly, "dream of your eyes."

He turned to his escorts. "Remove your crystals."

Each guard reached to their necks, pulling away small crystals hung on leather cords. The air around them shimmered like heat over summer stones.

Where three human guards had stood now towered three elves—tall, elegant beings with luminous skin and pointed ears. Their eyes held centuries.

Sido smiled, a mystery solved. But Shandar backed away, terror flashing across her face. Her hands erupted in flame—not the wild bursts of before, but concentrated fire that coiled around her fingers like living snakes.

"Elves," she gasped, flinging one hand out defensively.

A fireball blasted through the air, missing the nearest elf by inches and burning a perfect circle through the wooden door.

Sido stepped between them. "Breathe, child. They mean no harm."

The flames didn't die but gathered tighter around Shandar's hands, ready to strike again.

Blair approached slowly, hands raised. "Shandar," he said, using her name with careful emphasis. "They are my allies. My friends."

The flames flickered, uncertainty crossing her face.

"Can you control this fire well enough to travel?" Blair asked, his voice gentle but direct.

Shandar shook her head, eyes haunted. "It comes when I'm afraid. When I'm angry." She looked at her hands. "I can't always stop it."

Sido moved to her side. "Magic obeys intent before skill. Picture what you wish to do, then believe in it."

Shandar closed her eyes, shoulders tense with concentration. The flames receded slightly, dancing closer to her skin.

A knock rattled the door. Shandar's eyes flew open in alarm. Her arm shot forward reflexively, another fireball punching through the already damaged wood.

Landon stumbled through, his sleeve smoldering. "I nearly lost my head!"

"Are you hurt?" Sido asked, examining his arm.

"They didn't warn me they were practicing destructive magic in here," he muttered, eyeing Shandar's armor with sudden recognition. He bowed hastily. "The Council awaits, Head Mother."

Sido positioned herself to block his view of the elves. "This cannot be rushed," she said firmly. She turned to Blair. "Stay with her. Share everything you know of the prophecy."

To the tallest elf, she added: "Prince Finrod, I beg you to consider her need for training before you depart at dawn."

The elf inclined his head gravely.

"If this prophecy fails," Sido said, her final words heavy with centuries of knowledge, "even the elves will struggle to survive what comes." She met Finrod's ancient eyes. "Think on that before you send a half-trained fire mage stumbling into the wilderness."

The door closed with a soft click.

Silence settled over the chamber like dust. Shandar's bones pressed against the wooden chair, her knuckles white against the worn armrests.

"You're elves," she said, the words harsher than intended.

Finrod's silver-blue eyes, ancient as winter ice, flickered as he dipped his head. His gaze revealed nothing—a frozen lake unmarked by footprints.

Violet sparks arced between Shandar's fingertips, crackling in the quiet. "What quest are you dragging me into? What are we hunting?"

The other elves exchanged a glance so swift she nearly missed it. In the hearth, flames roared, casting restless shadows across the walls.

The metal cuffs at Shandar's wrists creaked as she shifted.

Blair rose, each step heavy with reluctance. His chest rose and fell in shallow bursts. "Mistress…"

"Shandar," she cut in, chin lifting. "I'm as much a mistress as I am dead."

He swept dark hair from his forehead, exhaling. "Shandar." He began pacing, two sharp strides, pivot, his gaze darting from floor to windows to her face. "I was hired to guide them to Dragon Rest. I sought a talisman that led us to Tartus, above Talon Pass."

Ice flooded her veins at the name. Tartus. The creature Sido whispered of in the darkest corners of her teachings, never in daylight.

"That's where he stripped away our disguises," Blair continued, voice tightening. "Where the prophecies were spoken. We came seeking the Mistress of Fire. Now you stand where we stand, blind at the edge of an abyss."

The knot in Shandar's throat burned. "You mean Sido's poem? And Tartus, what is he?"

Finrod stirred. "Your human version is but a splinter of truth."

"Why does time matter so desperately?" Shandar pressed.

Blair's head snapped toward Finrod, naked alarm in his eyes.

The room grew still. Finrod closed his eyes. His hand thrust into empty air and emerged clutching a tiny grimoire no larger than his palm. Its leaf-thin pages pulsed with unnatural rhythm, like something alive.

"This," he whispered, voice dropping to thunder, "is the elvish prophecy."

He spoke a single word, "Edro."

The book sprang open. Sickly green light bathed his angular features, turning them skeletal. His voice rolled out: "When Fornax, Horologi, and Triangul align with Izar, our doom is sealed."

He rose abruptly, pacing the hearth's rim. Three measured steps, turn. His shadow stretched impossibly tall against the wall.

"You know them as the Furnace, Clock, Triangle, and the Raiment. Within this season, they converge." His voice darkened. "No mortal has witnessed this alignment and lived."

The chamber grew so cold Shandar could see her breath. Finrod halted at the hearth's edge, drawing air like a drowning man.

"The Dragon Rest mountains sprawl across the horizon like a burning spine. Time hunts us. Danger stalks us." His voice faltered. "Triangul's tip already pierces the night sky."

His composure cracked. He sat, then jerked upright as if the chair had burned him, naked fear flashing across features too perfect for human expression.

The book closed with a soft, mournful sigh that seemed to echo from a distant grave.

"How long?" Shandar's voice arose as brittle ice.

The three elves shared a look of grim resignation. Blair's restless hands fell still.

"Weeks," Finrod finally said, each word a stone on a tomb. "Perhaps less."

CHAPTER 9

SEEKING PASSAGE

Rika woke to a hand crushing her windpipe. She couldn't breathe.

Her fingers scrabbled beneath her pillow, found the dagger's hilt. She stabbed upward, blind with panic.

Strong fingers caught her wrist mid-strike. "Shh." Merric's breath warmed her ear. "It's me. We have visitors."

The pressure eased. Recognition flooded her as she went limp, heart hammering against her ribs.

He pressed the knife back into her palm. "Corner. Now. Silent." Each word clipped, urgent. He shoved her into shadow, then stuffed pillows beneath the blankets to mimic sleeping bodies. The doorknob squeaked. Merric's finger pressed against his lips.

Rika's vision blurred. The room tilted. A cold sensation washed over her as her consciousness split, part of her remained pressed against the wall, Merric's arm a barrier before her, while another part drifted upward.

From the ceiling, she watched as the door swung open. A man slipped in, silent, predatory. Moonlight caught his blade.

I'm going to die, thought the Rika below, while the Rika above watched, detached yet terrified.

The assassin raised his knife. As it descended, Merric lunged from the shadows. His sword punctured the man's side with a wet, terrible sound. The intruder gasped once. His body convulsed, then went still.

Rika snapped back into herself with a violent jolt that left her gasping.

Merric darted to the door, checked the hallway, then returned to the corpse. He brushed back the dead man's hair, revealing a small tattoo behind the ear. His face hardened.

"Pack. Boots. Now."

He disappeared into the privy. Retching sounds followed. Rika pulled on her boots with trembling hands, grabbed her pack, and approached the door. "Are you…"

His hand clamped over her mouth again. His eyes, when they met hers, were fierce but shaking. A killer's eyes that had never killed before.

Outside, Rika's spirit tore free again, this time without her willing it. She hovered near the ceiling, watching Merric guide her empty-eyed body down the corridor. At each landing, he paused, listened, then moved on with the precision of a man hunted.

In the common room, a gray-striped cat lifted its head from the bar. Rika's astral form drifted toward it. When she touched its fur, the cat purred, arching its back. Her physical body blinked, disoriented.

Merric cracked the front door. "Left. Water barrel. Watch for guards."

In the alley, they crouched in darkness. Smoke drifted across the street. Merric threw out an arm, blocking her. Above them, Rika's spirit saw what they could not—two men with knives waiting in the shadows across the way.

She crashed back into her body, gasping. "Two men. Knives. Opposite alley."

Merric's eyes widened, but he didn't question her. He tapped her wrist, then pointed: cross there, turn left, docks.

Her spirit rose more easily now as they darted from shadow to shadow. It felt like swimming through cool water while her body moved below.

The River Rat waited at the pier, a fifty-pace sloop, single-masted. A sailor stood watch, bored and drowsy. Rika's spirit hovered over the water. On impulse, she flicked at the man's earlobe. He slapped at it as if bothered by a gnat. A tingling sensation shot through Rika's physical hand.

Merric tossed a gold coin that caught the lantern light. "My fare is paid."

The sailor caught it, nodded, and lowered the rope barrier. They slipped behind the cabin, where Merric helped Rika settle back into her shivering body.

"He moved wrong," Merric whispered, staring at the worn planks. "Weight forward, never hovering. That's how I knew." His voice cracked. "He would've killed you if I'd woken you normally." His hands trembled. "I've never taken a life before."

"When you stabbed him, I wasn't there," Rika said, the words tumbling out. "I was above, watching. That's why I made no sound." She paused, testing his reaction. "I can leave my body. See things. Places I shouldn't be able to see." Another pause. "I always thought it made me evil. Tonight it saved us both."

The lantern light softened Merric's features. "The mark behind his ear, a bounty mark. You're wanted." He reached toward her face, then withdrew. "How do I keep you alive until we find the prince?"

She hesitated, then whispered, "Only the Queen knew of the bounty. And the King. The man who placed it…" her mouth twisted, "…Saad put it there when I refused him. He forced a kiss, called it honor." The word tasted bitter.

Merric's eyes darkened. "Saad." He spat the name like poison. "He feeds on fear. No one in the guard trusts him." He scrubbed his hands against his thighs as if trying to wipe them clean. "Rest now. Dawn's hours away."

They leaned against the cabin wall, shoulder to shoulder, as the River Rat slipped into the current, carrying them from danger into darkness.

Evening shadows crept across the stone chamber walls like living things, the sputtering torches barely holding them at bay. Five figures sat around an ancient oak table, its surface scarred by weapons and time: Shandar, fingers still smoldering with ember; Finrod, the elf lord, his midnight-blue cloak stark against pale skin; Head Mother Sido, silver braid coiled over one shoulder; Kumar, armor dust-stained from the road; and Blair, the young prince, white-knuckled around a golden medallion.

Between them lay scrolls with flaking ink and half-eaten bread on chipped plates. Water dripped somewhere in the shadows, each drop echoing like a tiny heartbeat.

Blair broke the silence first. "This prophecy, Mother Sido, what does it mean?" He pushed a weathered tome toward her, its binding cracked with age.

Sido smiled, then nodded to Finrod. The elf rose with fluid grace, his ear brushing his shoulder as he bowed. "Tonight we honor human scripture," he said, voice like distant bells. "Mother, proceed."

Sido opened the book. The scent of old parchment and incense rose from its pages. Her finger traced the words. "'Mistress of Fire, Seeker of Stone.'"

Her eyes flicked to Shandar, whose spine straightened.

"Shandar commands flame," Sido said. "The elves seek the power-stone."

Shandar's lips parted. Embers flickered at her fingertips. Around the table, heads nodded.

"'Reflection in the Eyes of Demon Unknown,'" Sido continued, frowning. "A being twisted by Gwydion's Making."

Finrod's eyes gleamed. "Our lore speaks of a dragon," he said, each word falling like stone. "Ancient. Patient. Cold as obsidian."

"A dragon?" Shandar's voice cracked. The sparks at her fingertips leapt higher.

Blair's shoulders slumped as if crushed by an invisible weight. "Dragons are myths. Six centuries gone."

"Your ancestor banished it," Finrod said, meeting Blair's gaze. "King Willow. The dragon has waited. It returns seeking vengeance."

Blair paced, footsteps hollow against stone. "How powerful is such a creature?"

"A dragon's fury turns towns to ash," Sido said quietly. "Heart, home, spirit, all consumed."

Silence fell, broken only by water dripping in darkness. Blair sank into his chair, head in his hands. "And to banish it again?"

"No one knows," came the reply, multiple voices speaking as one.

Shandar's whisper was almost lost beneath the torch's sputter. "Dragons... real."

Blair rubbed his temples. "The rest of the prophecy?"

Sido turned the page. "'Loins of royalty hold the key.'" Her finger trembled. "You, Your Majesty."

Finrod leaned forward. "Elven blood matters, but your aura burns brightest."

A blush crept up Shandar's neck. "I sense it too. Such power in you."

"'Only triumph shall set the nations free,'" Sido continued.

Blair covered his face. His shoulders rose and fell with a shuddering breath. His shadow stretched across the ceiling, a king's crown or executioner's axe.

"'Castle builders deal with stone,'" Sido read. "Giants from the mountain forts."

Finrod gazed upward as if seeing through stone. "Giants measure time in decades, not days. Their walls endure."

"'Golden Heart and friend to all,'" Sido whispered, eyes closed. "A healing knight of pure spirit."

"A fairy warrior," Shandar said, determination hardening her voice.

"'Seven to seal the dome,'" Sido finished. "Seven souls or seven deeds forming a dome of magic."

Finrod closed the book with reverent hands. "These words point to events yet unfolding. We must move while the path remains clear."

He outlined their plan: Blair and Kumar would ride at dawn for the Astar Hills seeking Aurin Sweetwater, keeper of giant and fairy lore. Shandar would train under Sido. Finrod would search the library's deepest vaults.

Blair's smile was grim but determined as he lifted his chin. "First light, then. Half a moon's time, or not at all."

Outside, the torches guttered. Stars peered through the high window, silent witnesses as prophecy's gears began to turn.

The patrol burst from the Wine Forest's dense shadows into blinding sunlight. Andreas raised a hand against the glare, squinting toward the Tribute River that glinted like a silver thread in the distance. King Vardon's orders haunted him: scout for Morag forces. But every heart-beat brought back the sound of the arrow that felled Tomas beside Prince Saad. Guilt tightened around Andreas' chest like a vise.

In the column's center, Saad's horse danced nervously beneath him. "Commander," the prince called, voice cracking. "Please... Adanna. Let us rest at Adanna."

Andreas clenched his jaw. He recognized the naked fear in Saad's eyes because it mirrored his own. Still, he forced out the words: "Your Highness, we ride on." Each syllable tasted like ash.

They crested the rise. A lone Morag lurched into view, flesh flayed, crimson ichor dripping from open wounds. Two riders surged forward, but the creature bolted past, eyes wild with terror.

"Report!" Andreas barked at Cohen and Andrew. Their vacant stares toward the valley chilled his blood.

Heart hammering, he urged his mount forward. At the summit, he froze.

Below, death marched across the plain. A living tide of Morag warriors spilled across the valley, backed by towering Aloiene wielding pikes and axes. Sixty thousand strong, at least. Andreas' mouth went desert-dry. Each breath felt stolen from the dead.

"Cohen," he managed, voice strangled. "Ride for Adanna. Warn them." He swallowed. "Andrew, to the king. Diamond formation! Protect the prince!"

He wheeled, expecting Saad's silhouette. The prince was gone.

Panic surged through him as he spotted Saad spurring his mount up the exposed slope. "Saad! No!" The words tore from his throat, swallowed by distance.

An Aloiene's roar answered, the massive creature locking onto the solitary rider.

Something snapped inside Andreas, cold, furious clarity. He drew his sword, the blade catching sunlight like fire.

"Forward!" he shouted, voice raw with purpose. "Protect him!"

The words hung in the air as his men hesitated, torn between duty and survival. Andreas didn't wait. He spurred his horse toward the prince, toward certain death, toward the only choice he could live with, or die for.

CHAPTER 10

THE RIVER RAT

A sharp breeze rattled the River Rat's rigging. The waning moon cut the sky like a knife, offering little light through roiling clouds. Rika leaned against the cabin wall, counting each hour like a wound. Two days on this boat, and the relentless slap of water against the hull had become the rhythm of her fear.

Merric crouched at the rail, one hand never far from his knife. His gaze swept the shoreline where reeds whispered secrets.

"Why you?" Rika finally asked. "Why would the Queen trust a huntsman to escort me?"

Merric didn't turn. "I tracked Blair for eight seasons before he learned to hide his trail." His leather jerkin creaked as he shifted. "I'd know him blindfolded in a crowd of thousands."

"And me? Am I dangerous? Because of what I can do?"

Now he turned, torchlight catching in his beard. "The Queen believes you may prove valuable." His eyes narrowed. "That's enough for me."

"But not enough for you to sleep," Rika observed.

A shadow moved behind them. Merric's knife appeared in his hand before Rika could blink. The sailor froze, then retreated without a word.

"How far to Blair?" she asked when her heart slowed.

"Riop, then Tiereny if we're lucky." Merric sheathed his blade. "Rest. I'll keep watch."

Rika lay beneath the stars, cold seeping through her cloak. The memory of her last vision clung to her, flames dancing inside her lungs, blood writing omens into her bones. She couldn't forget. She didn't want to.

Her chest tightened.

The rift opened.

Not peace, never peace. Her vision smeared. Her mouth filled with metal and heat. She choked as her spirit tore loose from flesh.

Above the deck, wind keened against the rigging. Her spirit hovered, trembling. Burke slouched at the tiller, flask limp in his grip. She drifted toward him, rage pulling her like gravity.

The scent of brandy reached her, a reminder of every night he'd watched her, every comment about her breeches.

"DRUNK." The word left her not as sound but as force.

Burke's head snapped up. The tiller spun. The mainsail buckled with a crack, and the ship veered toward land.

The tree loomed, massive and ancient.

Wood shattered. The impact slammed Rika's body from the wool. Pain rang through both forms, flesh and spirit.

Then hands, rough, urgent. A grip on her shoulder. Merric.

She collapsed into herself like the wake of thunder.

Her breath came in pieces.

Merric knelt beside her, his face pale with concern. But she couldn't speak yet. Not with fire still boiling beneath her tongue and the echo of Burke's shame lodged behind her ribs.

"The sailor," she managed.

"I know."

On deck, Burke lay against the broken tiller, blood trickling from his temple. Captain Mossman appeared, his face a thundercloud.

"She did it!" Burke slurred, pointing. "She screamed in my head!"

Mossman hauled Burke to his feet, then hurled the flask into the river. "Off my ship, you drunken fool!"

Burke followed his flask overboard with a splash. Mossman turned to Rika and Merric, his decision final. "Find another way to Riop."

Dawn found them trudging along the muddy riverbank, Burke stumbling ahead, clothes still dripping. Each step pulled at Rika's boots like hands trying to drag her under.

When Burke slowed, glancing back with bloodshot eyes, Merric's knife appeared. Rika touched his arm. The blade lowered, but Merric seized Burke's collar.

"Ten paces behind us," he growled. "No talking."

They walked until dusk, when even Merric's determination faltered. They made camp beneath a stand of birches. Burke huddled at the edge of firelight, shivering.

When he crept closer to the warmth, Merric's blade flashed. A thin red line appeared on Burke's wrist. The sailor retreated, muttering curses.

They reached a ferry dock as the sun dipped low, a ramshackle shack beside a weathered pier. The ferryman squinted at them.

"Spray leaves at sunrise," he grunted. "Deck passage only."

Merric tossed silver onto the counter. Rika added gold. "A room," she said, her voice leaving no room for argument.

Upstairs, Merric checked every corner, then barred the door. "Rest," he said. "I'll wake you when it's time."

Hoofbeats shattered the silence. Merric was at the window instantly, knife in hand. Two riders approached, torches blazing. The lead rider pulled back his hood.

"Merric..." The name left his lips like an echo of memory.

Rika's heart pounded as she and Merric descended toward the firelit clearing. There, beside the horses, Prince Blair waited, his eyes unreadable in the shifting light.

Before thought could intervene, Rika dropped to one knee. Training overruled emotion.

Blair's hand on her shoulder felt impossibly light. "Stand," he murmured. "I travel in shadow."

Inside, Blair's gaze settled on her, cool and perceptive, as if reading a text written in her bones.

Rika straightened her spine. "I am Rika Gresso. Your mother's newest maid." Her breath hitched. "I discovered I can leave my body. Move unseen. At first, I thought it a curse."

Blair's expression didn't change, but his eyes did, light catching curiosity.

"And now?"

"Now I see it has purpose."

A breath of silence. Then Blair smiled, brief but real. It softened his features, peeled away layers of crown and burden.

"My mother chose well in Merric," he said, "though she owes him an apology. A huntsman shouldn't carry a knight's burden."

They shared a meal, but Blair's face darkened as he spoke.

"War looms," he said quietly. "A death at the Making ceremony was only the spark. The Mistress of Fire has been found. We follow the Regin of Fire prophecy" His fingers tightened around his cup. "I didn't seek this path. It's been placed beneath my feet."

He turned to Rika. "Show me."

Rika shut her eyes. Her breath slowed. The world fell away.

Amber light flared around her, molten. Her spirit unmoored.

When she returned, gasping, Merric was already there, water ready, patience steady.

"Burke was listening outside," she whispered.

Blair nodded to Kumar, who vanished with silent efficiency and returned just as quietly, Burke secured.

Then something fractured.

Blair ran a hand through his dark curls, his posture sinking. His features turned younger. Less prince, more boy.

"As heir, I was taught how to govern," he said. "Not how to survive this." His voice trembled. "I trained for order. Not for fire."

Rika watched the shift in him, fear wrapped in resolve. Still, he reached toward her, not in touch, but in purpose.

"Come with me," Blair said. "Your gift may turn what's hopeless into what's possible."

Rika bowed her head. Words dissolved in her throat as fear and conviction braided inside her chest.

She didn't know what path lay ahead. But in that moment, she knew she would follow it.

Blair turned to Merric. "You must ride to the capital. Cancel the bounty on Rika's head and warn my father."

Merric nodded, determination hardening his features. "I will. And I'll see her safely returned when this is done."

Blair rested his hand on his sword hilt. "We ride for the Aster Hills, to seek Aurin Sweetwater. The knowledge of giants and Fairy may be our only hope now."

The fire had dimmed to embers. Blair's profile, once crisp against the dusk, now blurred into shadow. But Rika still saw the echo of his words, etched in the space between them.

He hadn't commanded. That was what lingered.

Not "You will" or "You must."

Come with me.

She sat apart from the others, knees drawn close, cloak pulled tighter as the night deepened. The stars blinked above like watchful eyes.

For so long, her life had been a thread woven beneath others' hands. A maid. A spy. A ghost in corridors. She'd learned to be invisible by necessity, not choice. Now her gift, the curse she once feared, had been named useful.

Worse, important.

The weight of that terrified her.

And yet... Blair's voice had held vulnerability, not demand. The way he'd looked at her, not through her, but into her. As if she weren't just a tool, but someone who might matter.

She pressed her palms together and leaned her forehead against them, steadying her breath.

She hadn't answered him, not really. A bowed head could mean many things.

But in her chest, beneath the trembling, something fierce had begun to form. Purpose not assigned but chosen.

She would follow him. Not because he was the prince. Not because the Mistress of Fire protected the realm.

But because when he asked, he left room for her to refuse.

And that, that was worth answering.

CHAPTER 11

TRAINING AND TRUST

Sido's patience felt sacred. Three weeks into her merciless regimen, Shandar found herself secretly clinging to the Head Mother's unwavering calm, though pride barred her from admitting it. The meditation chamber pressed in on her, a claustrophobic cube of unyielding stone with no windows, barely wide enough for her to stretch her arms without grazing the walls. A single white candle, barely two hands high, sat unlit on a rough-hewn desk. The air was thick with the scent of beeswax and the sharp tang of latent magic, as if the very stones exhaled power.

Shandar inhaled sharply, frustration coiling in her chest. Sweat glistened at her temples despite the cold. "Seven hells," she spat under her breath.

"Again," Sido's voice rippled through the stillness, calm as a hidden pool. "Fill your lungs completely, then release until you can barely draw another breath." She moved through the exercise with measured precision, chest rising, falling, a quiet testament to control. "Yes. Let go."

Shandar mimicked the motion, hands clasped so tightly behind her back that her knuckles burned white. Every muscle in her shoulders screamed. She dared to glance at the candle. "Why does fire obey me so easily when I'm angry," she asked, voice tight, "but vanish when I need even a single spark?"

Sido inclined her head, eyes thoughtful. "Your gift is extraordinary. At your age, most struggle for years to glimpse the spiritual plane, yet you slip between worlds as if drifting through a dream. Tell me, how did you learn this?"

Shandar's gaze fell to the flagstones. Memories flickered, her mother's gentle hands guiding her first breath into the void. She swallowed, voice barely more than a tremor. "I... my mother taught me when I was very young. That's all."

The truth hung between them and Sido's next question died on her lips. The Head Mother's stern nod sent Shandar's heart pounding, both relief and guilt washing over her. "Very well. Now, produce fire, just enough to light that candle." She inclined her head toward the desk.

Eyes closing, Shandar reached for the spiritual plane. It welcomed her like an old friend, a warm pulse at the base of her skull. She opened her eyes, raised her arms, and watched golden flames crackle to life along her forearms. The sensation was a familiar hum, an extension of her very soul.

Just light the candle. Nothing more.

She willed the flame forward, wrist flicking, and disaster. Magic surged beyond her command. The desk flipped backward with a thunderous crack as candle and stone collided against the far wall. A fissure spidered through the ancient rock. Through it, a young acolyte's face appeared, eyes wide and terrified, dust clinging to his hair.

Horror seized Shandar. Flames winked out as abruptly as they'd come, leaving her knees sinking into stone. She wrapped her arms around herself, trembling. I could've killed him.

Sido smoothed her robes, face unreadable save for the faintest parting of her lips. After a long moment she spoke, quiet as dusk. "It will come. Soon this will be second nature. You're closer than you think." She bent to lift Shandar to her feet. "Now go eat. You'll need strength for combat training."

The training grounds loomed ahead an hour later, discipline and exhaustion forging chains around Shandar's limbs. Morning sparring with Finrod and Arbor, afternoon lessons with Sido, her days blurred into a relentless beat she feared she could not sustain. Still, she pressed on. Blair's selfless dedication had awakened something fierce and protective in her heart. And Irit's death during the Making haunted her nights, screaming in her dreams. Mastering her power wouldn't bring Irit back, but maybe it would make her sacrifice mean something.

She almost turned away, but memories of Blair's determined gaze, of Irit's final scream, propelled her forward.

At the temple's edge, Finrod and Arbor stood waiting. Finrod held out a gleaming bundle. "From now on, you train in this armor," he said, voice cool and uncompromising. "You must learn its weight, its limits."

Shandar took the bundle with a stiff nod. "No need to whisper in Elvish," she muttered. Finrod's expression didn't soften. "It is time, Mistress."

Behind a vacant stall, she donned the leather-and-steel embrace that hugged her form like a second skin. A surge of power bloomed within her, sweet and intoxicating. Surfacing into the sunlight, she startled a stable hand into a wall and sent a maid's linens fluttering to the ground. Heat flamed her cheeks; she resolved to find a cloak.

Finrod produced a sleek black rod. "And this?" he asked. He pressed her hand to a small bump and the rod extended, an elegant staff balancing perfectly in her grip. "Now collapse it again." She obeyed, and it shrank back. "Keep it at your thigh. Live with this staff as part of you."

She circled, staff strapped in place. Arbor sprang from the shadows like a silent arrow. Instinct took over: thumb clicked the staff into length, and she swept low. Arbor flipped over the blow and resumed his assault. She blocked, feinted, but mis stepped, and Finrod closed in behind her.

Panic roared through her veins. She spun, staff carving a circle of flame that erupted into an infernal wheel. The gust hurled both elves backward across the dust, raining fire in flaming ribbons.

Time slowed. She slipped into the kata Finrod had drilled into her, each posture fluid, each muscle attuned to the fire's dance. Arbor and Finrod retreated, circling warily.

Arbor rose, staff in hand. Without glancing, Shandar sensed his movement. She pivoted, arm outstretched, and a ribbon of flame curled from her fingertips, encircling his neck. The crystal he wore, shrouding his true self, shattered in green shards. Silver-white hair spilled free, ears elongated beneath the sun.

"STOP!" Sido's voice cut like a blade. The fire vanished, breath returning to the air in one soft exhale.

Shandar dropped to her knees beside Arbor, voice shaking. "Are you, are you all right?"

He managed a tired smile as he pushed himself up. "I am. Now I see why they call you Mistress of Fire."

Sido appeared at her side, robes unblemished by dust. "No lasting harm done. Arbor will heal quickly," she said, eyes both stern and proud. "Your precision was extraordinary. How did you do it?"

Shandar tugged at her collar, conscience raw beneath every gaze. "I... I lost myself in the flow. It became instinct." She bit her lip. "But I struck a friend. How do I guard against hurting those I care for?"

Finrod bowed his head. "Head Mother, forgive our intrusion. We pressed her too soon."

Sido's lips curled in a small, knowing smile as she turned back to Shandar. "Power without restraint destroys everything you love. You must forge an inner sanctuary, a still point in the storm that anchors you to reality." She pressed a hand to Shandar's shoulder. "Rest now. Eat. Meditate on this lesson. We will speak again."

Shandar bowed and left the arena with measured steps. Finrod and Arbor fell into formation beside Sido, watching her silhouette recede.

That evening in Adanna, one of only two unwalled cities in the kingdom, Valcom Ledwith supped with his wife, Judith, and their two daughters in a modest tavern by the window. The girls giggled as they lifted bowls of broth to their lips. Then, without warning, a blade wreathed in emerald fire shattered the glass and impaled the elder child. Her scream echoed once before a second wound silenced her forever. The younger girl's wail was cut short by the same green blade. Valcom's heart seized; he reached for them, only to feel the sword pierce his own chest. He sank, astonished by the swiftness of death, a mercy he could scarcely believe. Judith's fate in the ensuing horror would become the unspeakable legend of the night.

History would call it the Battle for Adanna, but massacre was the truer word. Hulking fiends, twisted half-breeds with inhuman strength, ripped through the streets, poleaxes glinting in torchlight. Green fire engulfed tim-ber-framed homes in seconds. Veteran guards, meant only as ceremonial honor, fell by the hundreds. Citizens fled toward the bay, only to find the invaders already forming a ring of steel and flame.

Stewart Seith Wedgewood ascended the roof of city hall, every scream and clash a hammer against his heart. He watched as crimson fire danced across the distant Wine Forest, then turned to the slaughter below. Desperation drove him to his study, where he scribbled a fevered plea for aid. With trembling hand, he tied it to a falcon's leg and released the bird into the stormy dusk. As the roof crumbled beneath him, his last prayer was that someone, somewhere, would hear this warning.

"The Mistress, the most powerful person who ever lived. Is this the other one from your dreams?"

Blair whipped around to face Kumar, his heart suddenly racing. Why would Kumar mention his dreams now? And why did Rika seem so familiar? Not in the same way as Shandar, whose fiery eyes still haunted him, but something else entirely. A sense of ease, of trust that defied explanation.

The forest path stretched before them, dappled sunlight filtering through the canopy. They'd been walking their horses for nearly an hour, giving the animals a rest before pushing on toward the Astar Hills. Blair glanced back toward Rika, who rode several paces behind. Her shoulders remained slumped since her tearful farewell with Merric at the dock.

He signaled Kumar to ride ahead, then guided Blaze alongside Rika's paint mare.

"How's that little filly treating you?" Blair asked, his voice gentle. The horse's coat gleamed with sweat from the morning's hard ride.

Rika stroked the mare's mane but kept her gaze fixed on the path ahead. "She's beautiful. Thank you for finding her for me."

"We were lucky to find her." Blair studied Rika's profile, noting the tension in her jaw. "I'm sorry about Merric. Sending him back was necessary, but I know he meant something to you."

The memory of their parting at the dock hung between them, Merric's protective embrace, Rika's shoulders shaking with quiet sobs as she walked away, Merric watching until she disappeared from view.

"Are you all right?" he asked, then at once regretted the inadequacy of his words. I'm not commanding you to be here. I want you to understand that.

Rika's fingers found the pendant at her throat. "I've had no one outside family care for me like that before. He saved me." Her voice cracked slightly. "I don't under-stand why he would risk himself for me."

She nodded once, composing herself. Blair urged Blaze closer, but Rika subtly shifted her mare, keeping the animal between them like a shield.

"That's how Merric is," Blair said, respecting the distance she created. "When he trained me, he always placed himself between me and danger, sometimes more than

I wanted. It's curious my mother chose him to escort you." He paused. "Do you know why she might have done that?"

"None whatsoever." Rika's fingers fidgeted with her reins, flicking them absently beneath her horse's neck. "I can only guess. He recognized you immediately when he saw you. I'd never met him before that night. He woke me and pulled me from the palace."

She gazed into the forest, her eyes reddening. "At first, he thought I was some troublemaker the Queen wanted removed. Then everything changed. He became... a friend when I needed one most." Her voice dropped to a whisper. "I've never felt so alone or afraid as I do now. What do you intend to do with me?"

When she finally looked at him, those eyes Blair found himself momentarily lost in their depths. I will protect you, he thought fiercely.

"I plan to keep you safe," he said, choosing his words with care. "Your talents will be invaluable to our quest finding the stones, defeating whatever guards them. If we succeed, people will have choices about their lives, not paths forced upon them by others." He guided Blaze slightly away, giving her space. "You'll have a choice in your future too."

"You're the Prince," Rika said, unexpectedly guiding her mare closer until their legs almost touched. "Surely you get to choose your own path?"

Blair laughed, the sound hollow even to his own ears. "That, Rika, is the one thing I don't get to decide. This quest was thrust upon me without a thought to what I wanted. The fates chose my path, not me."

"I don't see any guards forcing you to stay," she murmured. She clutched her horse's bridle for support, her knuckles white.

Blair closed his eyes briefly, exhaled slowly. "Speaking of dreams," he said, changing the subject, "do you remember yours?" *Fool. I should have asked directly if she's the other woman from my visions.*

"I rarely remember dreams for long," Rika replied after a moment. "Mostly I had daydreams imagining life as the Queen's maid, sometimes..." A flush crept up her neck. "Sometimes becoming a princess, finding true love like in the old stories." Her eyes met his briefly, something vulnerable flickering there. "Are your dreams troubling you?"

Blair rubbed the back of his neck, his gaze darting anywhere but at her. "They were haunting me, but they might have stopped." He hesitated. "Nothing unusual in your dreams lately?"

When she didn't answer, he couldn't tell if she'd shaken her head or simply remained still.

"You'll continue with us," he said more firmly, pulling himself straighter. "When we reach the Temple, Sido can properly assess your talent. A scout with your abilities will be invaluable." He sighed, feeling the weight of responsibility. "Our journey begins in the Astar Hills, where we'll meet a woman with knowledge of giants and fairies. She'll guide us to the other members we need for this quest."

Blair stepped between their horses, looking at Rika. Her proximity made his pulse quicken unexpectedly.

Rika stumbled, ending up standing before him, suddenly animated. "Giants and fairies? Like in children's tales? You're saying they're real?" Her voice dropped to a whisper, as if speaking too loudly might shatter some spell.

Blair's head tilted, a genuine smile warming his face for the first time that day. "I guess you'll have to come and see for yourself." The tension between them eased. "You don't need to ride behind us. Come forward and join the company."

They remounted for the next leg of their journey. Blair caught himself stealing glances at her. She is beautiful, he thought, then chided himself. I shouldn't look at her so much.

"I'll stay just behind, if you don't mind," Rika said, drawing a deep breath that she released slowly. "Giants and fairies... I need time to think about everything that's happening." Though she didn't look at him directly, a smile played at her lips, color rising in her cheeks.

She pulled on her reins, slowing her pace. Blair turned in his saddle to check on her...

Thunk!

An arrow embedded itself in the tree trunk inches from his head. Blair spun around, scanning the forest for the shooter. Protect her.

"Kumar! Arrows!" he shouted, already drawing his sword. A quick glance showed Kumar engaged with an attacker, blades flashing in the dappled light.

Blair leapt from his saddle, grabbing Rika's reins and pulling her horse close. "Down! Between the horses!" He crouched, peering over her saddle as another arrow whistled overhead. Two men came out from the forest to his right, but neither carried a bow. The shooter remained hidden.

"Take Blaze's reins," he instructed, pressing the leather straps into her hands. "Stay down and use your power. Find that archer and disrupt him somehow while I handle these two."

He unsheathed Comet, the blade catching sunlight as he strode toward the attackers. Behind him came a sharp crack of twigs. He pivoted, spotted movement, and lunged backward. In one fluid motion, he dived over Rika's crouched form, rolled across the dirt, and came up with his blade, slicing through the third attacker who'd tried to flank them.

The first attacker charged toward Rika. With no time to reach him, Blair hurled Comet. The sword spun end over end, then impossibly hung suspended for a heartbeat before plunging point-down into the earth before the attacker. Cornflower blue light erupted from the blade, throwing the man backward.

Blair vaulted over Rika again, rolled, and reclaimed his sword in one motion. The two remaining attackers converged.

He ducked beneath a wild swing, spun low, and swept the legs from under the man on his right. As the other brought his blade down, Blair blocked with Comet, pushed upward with both legs, and smashed the sword's guard into his opponent's face.

The attacker crumpled, and Blair drove his blade through the man's chest. The one on his knees recovered, a savage grin splitting his face. Blair circled right, feinting attacks to keep him off-balance. Then he broke left suddenly, leaping over the kneeling man. His opponent reacted quickly, thrusting upward, but his blade merely glanced off Blair's shoulder.

Blair slapped the attacker's weapon aside and drove Comet through his gut.

Breathing hard, he turned toward Kumar, who was leading his horse back, his own blade bloodied but the threat neutralized. Rika remained crouched between the horses, eyes closed, utterly still.

Blair sprinted into the forest. Several yards in, he found the archer sprawled on the ground, bow beside him, arm flung across his eyes, body trembling uncontrollably. Whatever Rika had done to him, the man was completely incapacitated.

"This one's yours," Blair told Kumar as he rejoined them, leaving the elvish warrior to deal with the archer.

Between the horses, Rika sat on the ground, her face ashen, eyes haunted. Blair gently took her under the arms and lifted her to her feet. The moment she registered his presence, she threw her arms around his neck, clinging to him as sobs wracked her body. He held her, one hand stroking her hair, his own breathing gradually slowing.

When her grip loosened, Blair carefully held her at arm's length, his hands steady on her shoulders. "Rika, can you continue? We need to move. There might be others looking for us." He gave her shoulders a gentle squeeze.

Her eyes met his, wide and vulnerable. As she looked at him, the tension visibly drained from her body. She turned her head away, then stepped forward to rest it against his chest.

"We should move." Kumar's voice cut through the moment, matter-of-fact and cold. "It's not safe here. I've disposed of the other one and hidden the body in the woods. Luthor, we must leave now."

Blair nodded, still holding Rika, feeling her trembling subside against him. Whatever connection was forming between them, it would have to wait. The path ahead was dangerous, and they had only just begun.

Blair found himself lost in Rika's presence, his duty momentarily forgotten. When he gently pushed her to arm's length, an ache spread through his chest. Part of him wanted nothing more than to let her find shelter in his embrace for as long as she needed. Her eyes, still glistening with tears, met his. He brushed away a linger-ing droplet with his thumb, offering her a smile that felt too small for what he wished to give.

"We need to move," he said, his voice softer than intended. "May I help you up?"

He cupped his hands to form a stirrup. Rika placed her palm on his shoulder for balance, her fingers trailing down his arm as she positioned her foot. For a heart-beat, she gripped his forearm tightly before releasing it. The brief contact left his skin warm beneath his sleeve.

With practiced care, Blair guided her into the saddle. He watched as Rika straightened her back, squared her shoulders, and drew a steadying breath. The vulnerable woman who had sobbed against his chest had vanished, replaced by the composed courtier he'd first met. With-out a backward glance, she nudged her mount forward toward Kumar, who stood rigidly by the road, one hand on his sword hilt, eyes scanning the tree line.

Blair stared after her, unsettled by how quickly she'd masked her emotions. We each carry our burdens dif-ferently, he thought. Her composure, my compassion strengths and weaknesses both, depending on the moment. The weight of the crown medallion pressed against his chest beneath his tunic, a constant reminder of duty.

He retrieved his own horse, which had wandered several paces away, and swung into the saddle. By the time he urged his mount into a trot to catch up, Rika and Kumar were already deep in conversation about the safest route forward, as though the ambush and what followed had never happened.

CHAPTER 12

THE PRICE OF DUTY

Blair's small company pressed on through the gathering dusk, their weary horses' hooves clattering over a narrow track choked with brambles and creeping ivy. Each labored breath sent puffs of dust into the amber light as the sun slipped below distant ridges. At last, through the tangle of pines, they made out a lone cabin in a moonlit clearing: timbers blackened by weather, the sagging roof weighed down by moss, its shuttered windows staring blankly into the gloaming. In that half-light it could have been abandoned for years.

"This can't be right," Kumar muttered, clutching his sword hilt until the leather straps creaked.

Blair slid from his mount, joints stiff as iron hinges in winter. He ran a hand over Comet's ornately carved pommel. "Wait here," he ordered softly, voice low. Edging forward, he approached the door, then it swung open without a sound.

A tall, wiry woman filled the frame, two strides taller than Blair. Her hair, a drift of silver waves, fell to her chest in unruly curls. Deep lines furrowed her cheeks, but her bright eyes shone with a sharp, welcoming intelligence. She wore a simple gown of forest green, belted at the waist, the fabric catching the last glimmer of daylight. "Prince Willow," she said, voice warm and clear. "You and your companions are welcome." She lifted her chin, inspecting him as though weighing his honor. "I am Aurin Sweetwater."

Blair dipped into a formal salute. When his gauntleted forearm met hers, her grip was like leather bound in iron. "You're too kind, madam," he said, stepping back. "May we stable our horses first?"

"Of course," Aurin replied, stepping aside. "Return soon, I'll have something hot waiting."

Blair led Blaze across the clearing to a sturdy oak. Rika and Kumar followed, silent as owls. Once out of earshot, Blair's fingers fumbled with the reins. "She knows my name," he whispered, voice taut. "No ordinary hermit. Stay alert." Kumar nodded grimly; Rika's hand drifted to her dagger.

The cabin's interior matched its decrepit exterior, cold hearth, splintered chairs, cobwebs shrouding every corner. Aurin stood just inside the doorway, waiting.

"Come in," she said. The words hung in the air like a binding spell.

The moment Blair closed the door, the room transformed. Polished parquet gleamed beneath a crackling fire. Two velvet couches faced each other across a glass table on an oval rug of black and white. Blair and Kumar froze; Rika's breath caught. Aurin glided to the hearth and lifted the lid from a cast-iron pot. The rich aroma of pork-and-potato stew, laced with rosemary and garlic, filled the chamber. Fresh bread steamed on the windowsill.

"Sit," Aurin said, her smile not reaching her eyes. "I'll fetch bowls. Prince, the wine and glasses are in that chest."

She pressed a hidden panel in the wall, revealing a small alcove lined with shelves. Blair retrieved a dusty bottle and four crystal goblets, setting them carefully on the table. As Kumar and Rika seated themselves, Blair noticed how the elf's ears had sharpened to perfect points, his skin faintly glowing along delicate runes. Rika, still absorbing their surroundings, hadn't noticed.

Aurin returned with steaming bowls. She placed one before Blair, then settled beside him. "Eat," she said softly. "Only I can see this place as it truly is."

The stew melted on Blair's tongue, earthy potato, tender pork, a whisper of thyme. Midway through his second bite, his arm grew heavy, immovable. He set down his bowl with a clatter. "We came by Sido Byers's request, not to be manipulated." He tried to stand. Couldn't.

Aurin's hands swept in a slow arc. "Dangerous times demand caution." Blue light bloomed at Blair's hip, wreathed Comet's scabbard, and rippled across his body. The paralysis shattered.

Blair scrambled back, levering Comet free. "That sword is more potent than I knew," Aurin murmured, eyeing its cornflower glow. "Introduce me properly, then I'll release them."

Blair took a breath. "Kumar, Rika, this is Aurin Sweetwater." At his words, Kumar and Rika slumped forward, free again. Rika brushed off her blouse with a small huff. "Do you need to terrify everyone for hospitality?" she asked. Without missing a beat she added, "Your home is lovely. The stew is excellent." The contrast between her tone and her scowl was striking.

Aurin laughed, delighted. "I like your frankness. And you, elf, thank you for the release. You fought me well." She turned to Blair. "So, you found the Mistress. She fares well?"

Blair opened his mouth, silence came. He stared at his lips. He tried again; no sound emerged.

Aurin recoiled. "Attacked? By whom?"

Rika straightened. "Northmen," she said firmly. "When I touched one, I saw his daughter being roasted alive if he didn't kill Prince Willow. They came through the White Barrier north of the Waste."

Aurin's composure wavered. "The Barrier… myth. How did you learn this?"

"I read his mind," Rika replied coolly.

A tense beat passed before Aurin stood and faced her. "You're a witch."

Rika's eyes narrowed, then closed. Her body froze. Blair felt the air chill. Then her eyes snapped open. She stared at Aurin, accusing, and spoke without moving her lips. "She's a coward. She doubts her magic and fears death." She blinked, shook herself, and lifted her bowl.

Aurin's teeth ground together; her body trembled. When she regained control, she straightened her skirt. "I admire you," she said hoarsely. "Who are you?"

"Astral," Rika answered around a mouthful of stew. "Is that familiar?"

Aurin's eyes widened. "None have appeared in centuries. Prince, you're blessed with such an ally, and in such a form. Have you... bedded her yet?"

Blair's face darkened. "I'll ask you to show some respect. She is my companion by duty and by honor."

Aurin raised her palms. "No offense meant." She turned to Rika. "And you, Queen's Maid, how long have you traveled with him?"

"Since the new moon. I found him at the ferry."

"Then they haven't met," Aurin murmured, eyes gleaming. "I'd love to witness that." She rose, smoothing her skirts. "Giants are just code. You need Golden Heart and Friend to All, Dagmar, the fairy warrior. He'll answer only to the Mistress of Fire and her golden rule: treat others as you wish to be treated." She plucked a map from a shelf. "Search for hidden places: hollows under roots, gaps in stones. And have her touch him with her magic; let friendship guide you."

From a nearby table, she produced a delicate pendant. Rika caught it: a blue stone encased in white starbursts. "Star of Serenity," Aurin explained. "It shields your body from magic, lets your spirit wander safely. But your spirit itself remains exposed." She placed it in Rika's palm, folding her fingers around it. "Guard this with your life."

Dawn found them rested, if wary. Aurin stood in the doorway as they prepared to leave. "The shadows hide you from Northmen eyes," she said. "Make haste to the temple."

Blair bowed once. "We ride now," he told Kumar and Rika, voice pitched low. "Shandar must know what we've learned."

As they mounted their horses, Kumar leaned close to Blair. "Do you trust what she told us?"

"Not entirely," Blair replied, "but we have little choice."

Their breath clouded in the morning chill as they set off toward the temple, the weight of prophecy heavy on their shoulders.

Merric arrived at the palace as twilight gathered. Muffled voices carried through Queen Ellis's chamber door. He entered without knocking and found the royal couple huddled over a map, their faces drawn with worry.

Ellis looked up, hope flashing across her features. "Is Blair with you?"

Merric shook his head. The queen's shoulders fell as he relayed everything: the cabin, Aurin Sweetwater, the Star of Serenity, the Northmen's infiltration through the White Barrier.

King Vardon's face grew ashen. He pulled a silken cord by the hearth. Minutes later, Sholin A'Tai swept into the chamber, his silver-threaded robes catching the firelight.

"The prophecy speaks true, then," the wizard said after hearing Merric's account. His voice dropped to a near-whisper as he recited:

MISTRESS OF FIRE, SEEKER OF STONE

REFLECTION IN THE EYES OF DEMON UNKNOWN

LOINS OF ROYALTY HOLD THE KEY.

ONLY TRIUMPH SHALL SET THE NATIONS FREE.

CASTLE BUILDERS DEAL WITH STONE

GOLDEN HEART AND FRIEND TO ALL

WILL BE SEVEN TO SEAL THE DOME.

EVIL GROWS WITHIN THEM ALL.

DISTORTING THE PATH, THE MISTRESS CALLS

WITHIN EACH HEART LURKS DISASTER'S FACE.

ONLY DEATH OPENS THE GATE

MIXTURE OF SEVERAL TONGUES

COMES THE FREEDOM AND HOPE OF THE YOUNG

TRUE BELIEF IN COMPANION'S WORTH

IS ALL THAT'S NEEDED TO SAVE THE HEARTH."

"We must prepare," Sholin said finally. "Our lands will soon face forces beyond imagining."

Vardon straightened, his crown gleaming dully in the candlelight. "Then we defend what's ours." His voice carried the weight of generations of Willow kings. "Check the messenger cotes. Plan evacuation routes. Alert the border garrisons."

Ellis gripped the table's edge, knuckles white. "And Blair? What of our son?"

Sholin placed a weathered hand on her arm. "Your son walks the path the prophecy demanded, Your Majesty. And he does not walk alone." He turned to Merric. "The Queen's Maid, this Astral, she may be as crucial as the Mistress herself."

"I'll prepare scrolls," Sholin continued. "Ancient knowledge for Blair, and everything we know of Astrals for the maid." He fixed Merric with a penetrating stare. "Would you accompany them to Wund Mound at Nailk Lake? Few know its secrets as you do."

Merric nodded, surprised but resolute. "I serve the crown. And Blair."

"Then rest tonight," Vardon commanded. "You ride at first light."

As Merric bowed and turned to leave, he caught Ellis wiping a tear from her cheek, her queen's composure momentarily broken by a mother's fear.

Dawn cracked like bone against the horizon as Blair, Rika, and Kumar approached the Temple of Lashnar. The air tasted of singed cedar, smoke swirling low around the stables.

A flash of crimson split the morning mist.

Shandar moved like a storm given form. Her staff cut through the air trailing flame, her feet barely touching ground as she executed flawless combat forms. Each movement spoke of exhaustion hammered into precision, of power barely contained.

Rika halted her mount, transfixed. Shandar hadn't noticed them yet.

But when she did, her flames intensified.

A bolt of fire erupted from her staff, targeted and purposeful. It surged toward Rika with terrifying speed.

Comet appeared in Blair's hand as if called by blood. His blade intercepted the blast, steam hissing as magic met enchanted steel.

"Shandar!" Blair's voice carried command. "She's with us."

The flames vanished instantly.

Shandar lowered her staff, offering the barest nod that passed for acknowledgment. Her face revealed nothing—no apology, no regret.

Blair dismounted, his movements deliberate. Kumar helped Rika down, her pulse visible at her throat.

"Your forms have improved," Blair said, studying Shandar. "Less forced now?"

A hint of pride flickered across her features before she masked it.

"This is Rika Gresso," Blair continued. "Queen's Maid and Astral walker. We need her abilities."

Rika stepped forward, her curtsy precise—a perfect blend of dignity and formality that spoke of years at court.

"I've heard much about the Mistress of Fire," she said, her voice steady despite the lingering tension. "Perhaps as I discover my own abilities, we might learn from each other."

Shandar's eyes narrowed, assessing Rika with unsettling intensity. Something dangerous kindled in her gaze.

"Do all Queen's maids dress for the wilderness?" she asked, each word carefully weighted. "I expected some-one more... refined."

Rika didn't flinch. "And I can feel your power from here," she replied with glacial calm. "It makes the air crackle. Makes your hair stand like you've been struck by lightning."

Shandar stepped forward. The ground beneath her boots smoldered. Her staff remained unlit, but the threat was unmistakable.

"Enough." Blair's voice cut between them, not raised but final. The single word carried the weariness of someone who had expected this confrontation but hoped to avoid it.

Several heartbeats passed in strained silence before Shandar's posture softened. Then, with unexpected grace, she moved past Blair and embraced him.

"I worried," she murmured against his shoulder. "When you didn't return yesterday."

The vulnerability in her voice was genuine, startling in its contrast to her earlier aggression.

"Training alone has been..." she exhaled against his collar, "relentless."

Blair returned the embrace, though tension remained in his frame. As they separated, he caught Shandar's glance darting past him toward Rika, a look that mingled chal-lenge with something more complex.

He shifted subtly, positioning himself where he could see both women clearly.

Their expressions transformed simultaneously, forced smiles that didn't reach their eyes, poisoned honey coating steel.

Blair sighed and stepped back. "Show us to the kitchens," he said, resignation clear in his voice. "We have much to discuss, and daylight to waste."

As they walked toward the temple, Kumar fell in beside Blair. "That went well," he murmured dryly.

Blair's response was too quiet for either woman to hear: "This is only the beginning."

Above them, storm clouds gathered over the Temple of Lashnar, as if the very sky recognized the forces now assembled beneath it.

CHAPTER 13

A MOMENT OF PEACE

A cluster of silver-leafed poplars hid their camp from the road, the leaves whispering in the dusk breeze. They were two days' travel from the Temple, and tension between his two powerful companions had only sharpened. Blair leaned against a picket post, watching as Rika nudged her spirited mare so that it bumped Shandar's stallion. With a casual flick of her wrist, she dropped the reins and turned away, lips curved in challenge.

Shandar huffed, freeing her mount, which promptly kicked out, spraying fresh dung across Rika's buckskins. The splash of wet filth against leather made a sickening sound. Rika froze, shoulders stiffening as she whirled to face her rival, eyes widening at the spreading stain. She drew a long, measured breath, lips moving as though she spoke silent incantations, then found her voice. "Mistress," she said with a barely respectful nod. "Hard riding makes for short tempers." Her smile held a razor's edge. "Yet even in filth, your beauty is undiminished. Your armor hides nothing of your… gifts." She executed a perfect curtsy that threatened more than it bowed and strolled away. Shandar's hands lifted defensively, fingers splayed as if ready to conjure flames. Blair and Arbor exchanged amused glances as Arbor ran a gentle hand down Rika's mare.

"Better to tend horses than mediate those two," Arbor murmured. "This filly's bloodline is strong and proud, fortune smiled when she came to you."

Blair stroked Blaze's flank. "Prophecy," he whispered. "Some things simply fall into place." He pressed his forehead against the horse's shoulder, the weight of guiding two unpredictable mages bearing down on him. "They're like two cats with arched backs, touch one, and they'll both claw you."

Blaze shifted, and Blair straightened, weary of the charged atmosphere. "Arbor, entertain us no longer. Finish the pickets," he said, striding off and speaking soft Elvish as he went.

He kept his gaze on the path until he reached camp proper. There, Shandar stood with hands on hips, Rika with arms folded. For an instant they formed a united wall, then their eyes met, and they recoiled from one another as though burned. Blair slowed his breathing and adopted the grave, neutral tone his mother used to settle court disputes. "Ladies, the pace isn't too harsh, is it? We must press on. Is there a problem?"

They both began to speak but fell silent as Rika yielded. "We require greater consultation in party decisions," she said crisply. "Our counsel feels ignored."

Blair squared his shoulders. "I value every idea you offer. I promise to hear you out, but know that I alone decide what must be done and when."

Rika relaxed only slightly. Shandar cleared her throat as if to speak, but Blair held up a hand. "Rika, would you scout our surroundings with the Star? Report anything strange at once."

"I know how to use it," Rika replied coolly. "It's fundamental."

Shandar's foot tapped the ground. Blair placed a gentle hand on her shoulder. "Speak your mind."

Her voice was calm. "You're a prince, so you lead. But retrieving dragon-guarded stones by prophecy, you the best choice, or just the one with royal blood?"

"If I'd wanted command, I'd have stayed at court," Blair said, stepping back. "Finrod is a prince too, with centuries more experience. But this is my kingdom. I know its roads and people. I can move unseen, unlike you. Your power marks you."

"No one knows who I am," Shandar shot back.

Blair's lips curved in a rueful smile. "You and Rika are singular forces in this age. The prophecy names you, the Mistress of Fire. You must be guarded at all costs. I have brothers; my loss wouldn't break the prophecy. The elves have their own quest. One less elf prince won't derail things."

Shandar's whisper barely crossed the space between them: "It might break me."

He turned away, shoulders sagging. Then he faced her again, voice soft. "You're the most crucial person in this land. Without you, we can't face what's coming. Rika is the first Astral in centuries, no accident. Though not named, her gift of unseen scouting will save us from countless traps. The Northmen were just the start. It's not if we'll be attacked again, but when."

He glanced skyward. "Fables come alive. We don't yet know our enemy or how it strikes. Somewhere in the Dragon Rest Mountains, in a lair of legend, lie stones we must retrieve. We survive as a team, but when there's no time to debate, someone must decide. Fate chose me, and I've accepted that burden. I promise to listen, but in the end, I decide."

Both women straightened, chins lifting. Blair seized the moment: "Shandar, Kumar could use help with dinner. Trust me, it would be a kindness."

Surprise flickered on her face. She pressed a quick kiss to his cheek and strode to the cookfire. Rika, not to be outdone, grabbed Blair's hand. "Sit with me while I scout. Your presence grounds me in the astral currents." She led him to a fallen log by the flames. "Of course," he answered.

Rika slipped the Star pendant over her neck, fingers lingering on silver. She closed her eyes, palms warm in his hand. Blair felt Shandar's gaze as he withdrew his hand. When Rika opened her eyes, she met Shandar's pleased expression with a hard glance. From across camp drifted Finrod's soft laughter. "Fate knows its business," the elf prince murmured. "Most men would crumble between those two forces. You handled it with remarkable poise. Must be your mother's teaching, not your father's."

"My mother," Blair agreed. "Father left me to Glorin and Saad. I was an afterthought. Mother taught me to see the kingdom as she did. Rika and Shandar must now forge identities they never expected, to accept what they cannot change and believe in what they must do."

He watched the sky where stars blinked into being.

Rika's astral self, poured back into her skin like twilight spilling across a field. She blinked into waking, steadied by gasps and furrowed brows. Her smile was quiet, tender, more balm than bravado. Across the fire, Shandar sat rigid, arms crisscrossed like a fortress, her amber gaze sharp with calculation. The tension flexed between them, taut as a drawn bow.

Rika stepped forward, hand outstretched, not pleading, but purposeful. "We need to talk. Alone."

A flicker of hesitation passed through Shandar's face, but she took Rika's hand without a word. They slipped between huddled horses into a grove glazed in ash-gold firelight, leaves whispering overhead. When they settled knee to knee, the night held its breath.

Shandar's red hair flared like a warning beneath the embers. She placed her hands on Rika's knees, her voice even but distant. "Thank you. Blair must be clear-headed. Our quarrels muddle him. You conceding his heart is...gracious."

Rika's fingers curled around Shandar's with unexpected strength. "I didn't concede. We're not here for him. We need to talk about magic. And my feelings aren't up for negotiation."

Shandar pulled back sharply, arms folding like shutters. The warmth between them thickened, smoke without fire. Rika leaned into it. "You carry prophecy in your shadow. That kind of weight, how do you even breathe beneath it?"

Shandar stared into the dark beyond Rika, lips pressed thin. Chill crept into the grove like fog.

Rika continued, voice low and rooted. "I'm no chosen one. The stars skipped my name. But we're both raw. Unfinished. Sido gave you scripts and steps; I've had to improvise. Magic isn't a recipe. Its desire made visible."

She closed her eyes and reached inward, not to conjure but to believe. When her lids lifted, a fire-kissed butterfly hovered, wings shimmering with promise.

Shandar's guarded stare cracked. Her focus sharpened, and the butterfly erupted into a hawk, brilliant and consuming, wings slicing air with crimson flame. Rika flinched. Embers floated between them, trembling.

Silence grew roots.

"You're not what I thought," Shandar whispered. "I saw you as a distraction. Pretty and reckless. But you're something else. You care. Actually care. How did I miss that?"

Rika's throat tightened, the past blooming bitter in her chest. "I didn't know how to care. Not really. Until Saad."

She drew a breath like a bruise and let it go. "He hurt me. I reacted, instinct, not clarity. Merric was the aftermath. His kindness... real. He protects not because he must, but because he's made of it."

Shandar's posture softened. "And the Queen sent him?"

Rika nodded, brushing ash from her sleeve. "Old allies. She hid me after I struck Saad. Broke laws older than myths."

"She must be stunning," Shandar murmured.

Rika laughed, light through trees. "Compared to her, I'm weeds in cracked stone. She's grace carved in flesh. Her husband... less memorable."

Shandar leaned forward, brows furrowing. "You've met King Willow?"

Rika nodded, voice low. "Once. He burst in when I was with the Queen, tense, furious, storm trailing behind him. The room shrank around him. He wasn't expecting me."

Shandar's eyes narrowed with intrigue. "And Glorin?"

Rika shook her head. "No. They kept me tucked away, out of sight. Until Saad marked me."

Shandar stilled. "You're hunted?"

Rika shrugged, half-defiant, half-weary. "Most wanted, apparently. My face on scrolls, whispered in taverns. Saad doesn't forget."

Shandar's expression deepened, a mix of awe and calculation. "You're a wild card. My mother calls such people scale-tippers."

Rika leaned in, their knees touching. "I could show her. Project to her quarters if you describe them."

Rika tensed. "Would she welcome me?"

Shandar reined herself in. Then, gently, took Rika's hand. "She's a seer. Brutal and brilliant. I... disappoint her often. But you said belief powers magic. Explain that."

Rika smiled faintly, brushing hair from her brow. "It's like calling fire, you picture it, claim it, and mean it."

Shandar closed her eyes.

The air quivered.

And Blair appeared, bewildered, fork mid-air. "Well... I'm over here now."

He retreated to camp, eyeing them like a man caught between realms. "It's fine. I'll explain when I'm less startled."

Rika and Shandar exchanged a look, half amazement, half mischief.

Blair sat, resuming his meal. "So. Kidnapping mid-dinner. Charming."

Shandar's voice was crisp. "We needed you."

Blair narrowed his eyes. "You could've just asked."

Shandar's next words broke, raw. "Rika isn't in the prophecy. You and I survive. She might not."

Rika stared at her, heart thudding.

Blair wiped his mouth. "Prophecies aren't maps. They miss potholes and pitfalls. Any of us could die. A scared horse's hoof doesn't read omens."

Rika smiled gently. "That's why I trust you. You see what's real."

Blair's gaze darkened. "I'm terrified every step. I wasn't asked. I was chosen. And I don't know why."

Both women reached out, then pulled back as if scalded. Their rivalry breathed between them.

Blair stood, his exit abrupt.

Shandar vanished into the horses.

Rika stayed, ringed in embers and ghosts of connection, wondering if the fire they'd kindled would heal, or consume.

High sun beat down as they passed the once-empty King's Road to Escap, now crowded with travelers avoiding a rumored danger. Shandar's forest-green cloak billowed, Rika's new sky-blue tunic glinted in the heat. Cresting a rise, they spotted an ox wagon tilted on its side and a man and woman studying a broken wheel.

Blair raised his hand. "Need help with that?"

Finrod grimaced. "This is taking too long," he muttered. The wagoner stiffened, protecting his wife as they approached. Blair halted his mount; Rika and Shandar flanked him in a loose triangle.

Rika closed her eyes, breathing slowly. "Two children tucked beneath furs," she murmured. "They're moving household goods, starting fresh."

Shandar dismounted in one fluid motion. The man confessed he'd lost the lynchpin and had no spare. Shandar smiled. "Do you have any metal? We mean you no harm." He tossed her a belt knife. She caught and turned it in her hand. "This will do. Children, please come forward and step back."

Two wide-eyed kids came out. She extended her left arm. A whip of crimson flame lashed out, wrapping around the axle. The wagon rose six inches off the ground, the family gasping in unison. With her right hand, she guided a second band of fire, pushing the wheel back into place. Then, under her breath, she released the knife.

The metal blazed white-hot, its wooden handle falling away to ash. The blade twisted, melted, reformed and shot forward as a perfect lynchpin, slamming into place with a metallic ring. The wheel secure, she lowered the wagon gently to the ground.

The fire vanished with a snap. Shandar staggered, suddenly pale.

Little flair, why am I so tired? She thought. Reg would be proud, though.

Rika leaned down, voice warm. "You may go on now but spread word. Danger is coming. Find shelter, protect your family."

"Next you'll tell me elves walk among us."

Finrod slipped from his human guise; the others followed, revealing pointed ears and luminous skin. "We search for Dagmar now," he said. "Good forces gather. Tell all you meet."

The man fell to his knees as Blair drew his sword Comet, etched with his name, and held out the hilt. "Prince Blair Willow," he announced. The man bowed his head. Blair raised him gently. "Will you be all right?" The man climbed back into his wagon, dazed, and gripped the reins.

With a nod to Finrod, the party remounted and rode on toward the mountains.

A sudden whistle of arrows snapped the air. Blair shouted, "Ambush!" A nearby copse disgorged a dozen armed men. Shandar's horse reared as an arrow pierced its flank. She clung on, pale with shock. The elves loosed their bows; three attackers fell. Rika wheeled her mare to cover distance, numb with fear but precise. Blair found himself circled by three swordsmen. He parried, Comet clashing against steel, until a blade opened his thigh, he bit back a scream and fought on.

Shandar dismounted, staff aflame, spinning a fiery arc that felled two more foes. The stench of charred flesh filled the road. She staggered as the enemies died, face ashen, and retched. Arbor appeared as if from shadow and cut down an attacker. Blair dispatched the last man with a heavy stroke. Silence fell broken only by ragged breaths and skittish horses.

"Where's Rika?" Blair rasped. She rode up leading Shandar's rearing mount. He dismounted on his injured leg as she handed off the reins and knelt beside him. He pulled a scarf from his satchel and wrapped it around the gash. "Field kit in my saddle," he told her. "Will you stitch me up?"

Rika arched an eyebrow. "Perhaps Kumar…"

"Your hands are steadier. I've seen you embroider."

She caught his gaze. "All right." She drew a needle as Kumar brought the first-aid kit, mischief in his eyes. "Blindfold him?" he suggested quietly. Rika just smiled.

By midafternoon, they neared the crossroads where the Adanna and Escap roads met. A flood of refugees jammed the intersection, faces pale with panic. Stories of Adanna's destruction, walls burning, monsters of fire and brimstone, flowed from every waggoneer.

Fatigue and fear etched Rika's features; her breaths were shallow. Shandar's hood stayed drawn low, lips trembling. Blair's movements jittered with suppressed dread. He urged his mount forward to ride between Rika and Shandar. "Red Lion ahead," he said. "We need rest, clean clothes, a proper bed, and an ale, if I may."

Shandar met his gaze. "The prophecy warns of distorting the path the Mistress calls. Is that me or Lashnar?"

Blair nodded. "Just a warning. Prophecies are guides, not precise maps. They outline possibilities, not every detail. It could mean nature or karma, perhaps the entity Lashnar."

"Why so certain?" Shandar asked.

"Have you read Lanse Lexington's treatise on prophecy?" Blair began, voice calm despite the tension, ready to share yet another insight drawn from his mother's library. "The essence is what I told you: they provide frameworks, not specifics. We have our outline. We must trust ourselves to make wise decisions, focus on the destination rather than obsessing over interpretations. One step at a time."

As he spoke, the tension visibly eased from Shandar's shoulders. She smiled at him, warmth flooding her eyes.

"Blair," Rika interrupted, "you've been to the Red Lion before?"

Blair turned toward her. From the corner of his eye, he caught Shandar's scowl directed at Rika before she spurred her horse ahead to join Arbor.

"Twice," he replied. "Once as a young prince and once as Luthor the guide. They pay their staff and suppliers well and charge accordingly. The food is among the finest you'll find anywhere, and they serve a genuinely excellent house brandy. There are separate royal quarters, so availability shouldn't be an issue, though with so many travelers..." He left the thought unfinished.

As they topped a gentle rise, the Red Lion came into view, a three-story inn stretching three hundred paces along the road. Its once-bright red façade had weathered to a dull russet, save for the fresh paint on the shuttered stable gates. Blair frowned. "I've never seen those closed," he muttered. "Stay alert."

He called to Finrod, "We stop for food and rest tonight, but keep watch. Ladies, keep your cloaks until you're in your rooms, no needless attention." Finrod and Kumar positioned themselves around Rika and Shandar as Arbor brought up the rear. Blair hammered on the gate.

"Cleve! Let us in!"

A small peephole slid open to reveal suspicious eyes. The shutter slammed, chains rattled, and one gate cracked ajar. A square-built man with bloodshot eyes peered out. "Cleve's missing," he said flatly. "I only opened for you because you knew him. What do you want?"

"Lodging and food for the night," Blair replied, surprised by the hostility.

The man muttered about beggars overrunning the place if the gates stayed open, then agreed to stable their mounts. Finrod tossed him a silver piece; the man bit it, pocketed it, and bellowed for help before swinging the gates wide. "Nothing personal," he said with a wary bow.

Rika shivered as they entered. "Did things really get this bad?" she whispered.

Finrod slipped an arm around her. "It only worsens. Peace flees as evil stirs. Up north, near its lair, tranquility is unimaginable."

"She's going to its lair?" Rika's voice trembled.

Blair squeezed her hand. "To fight magic, you must face its source." He turned to Shandar: "Our identities and purpose stay secret."

He pushed open the heavy door. Darkness swallowed them until their eyes adjusted to the lamp-lit common room. Two carved lions flanked the entrance, their manes smoothed by years of superstitious hands. A warm, windowless hall stretched before them around a circular hearth.

At the far end, children of all ages sat rapt before a wordsmith's small wooden stage, laughter rippling through the hall. Even Shandar's vigilance slackened as the tale unfolded. "Children," Rika whispered. "Hope."

To their right, a polished bar hosted soldiers, merchants, and farmers. Three barmaids wove through the crowd. Along the entrance wall stood empty booths, except one, where a hooded figure watched them.

Blair led the group to the largest booth near the stairs. Rika offered to fetch their meal. As she approached the bar, two men eyed her. Then a tray-bearing woman appeared, froze at Rika's face, and called out, "Rika Grasso, the queen's maid without a queen, hiding from enemies?"

Rika stiffened. Karen Blankenship, the childhood tormentor, smiled with cruel delight. "Hot food and rooms?" she taunted.

Shandar intervened. She swept back her cloak, revealing armor gleaming like molten gold. The men at the bar stiffened. Karen sneered, "A she-cat warrior, sold off after all?"

Shandar's voice was calm but lethal: "Fetch Blair. No one needs to get hurt." Without warning, Karen's arms snapped to her sides, bound by invisible force. A bar towel flew into her mouth. The hall fell silent. Shandar's armor glowed with swirling flames that danced across her skin.

"I am Shandar, Mistress of Fire," she announced. "We're here to save this realm, don't insult someone you can't fathom." Her gaze swept the crowd. "She is worth more than all of you. Show us courtesy." With a thought, the towel and bonds vanished.

Karen collapsed back, gasping. Shandar added, "Six beds, dinner now, and provisions for dawn. We risk our lives for this land, be grateful." She paused. "One more thing: Rika can kill with a thought. Tread carefully."

Back at the booth, Shandar and Rika sat with their backs to the wall, flanked by Arbor, Kumar, and Finrod. The wordsmith's story resumed, quieter now. Blair returned, grim.

"Bernard's the innkeeper," he reported softly. "He had no rooms until I mentioned my name. We have royal quarters on the top floor, two rooms. I take one; Rika and Shandar the other. Three more rooms upstairs for the rest, plus a private parlor and dining room below."

Rika reached for Blair's hand. "Here," she said. "The children… they remind me why we fight."

Shandar nodded. "That laughter heals."

Before Blair could reply, servers arrived with steaming stew, roast chicken, fresh bread, and vegetables on fine platters. Crystal decanters bore wine and water. Each server bowed deeply and left.

Blair buried his face in his hands. "Does no one respect discretion?"

Finrod squeezed his shoulder. "Your name still inspires love. These people cherish their king." He tore bread. "Eat while we can."

In the shadowed corner, the hooded stranger signaled for another drink, eyes never leaving the unusual party.

King Vardon sat alone by the garden pool where his son had once attacked Rika. He hurled pebbles after pebble into the water, each ripple echoing his despair: useless, useless, useless.

He could not banish the scrying visions: a little girl's head, eyes wide with terror, floating amid walls liquefying into black sludge. Then carnage strewn through Adanna's marketplace, limbs, torsos, hands, followed by legions of warrior-mages. Even Sholin, his unflappable advisor, turned ashen.

"How can there be so many?" he'd whispered.

Vardon smashed a rock into the pool, shattering its surface. He'd sent falcons to Eastport with his decree: "Abandon your home. Flee with what you can carry. We cannot save you."

As the ripples faded, the water returned to its indiffer-
ent calm. King Vardon Willow, ruler of all Monde, felt
excruciatingly inadequate.

CHAPTER 14

WHISPERS OF WAR

Night was settling as the questers clustered in the Red Lion's royal sitting room, a vain attempt by local craftsmen to mimic true grandeur. Silk-draped walls, gilded mirrors, and painfully polished furnishings surrounded them. Blair flinched at the garish display, so far from the quiet dignity of genuine nobility.

"Send her away," he told the maid Bernard had posted outside. The door clicked softly, granting them privacy.

Kumar leaned against the window frame, his usual impassive face drawn tight. "The reports from the coast are worse than we imagined."

Arbor's voice was hollow. "No prisoners. The dark army slaughters everything in its path."

"Eastport next?" Blair's jaw clenched.

Kumar exhaled. "They're burning every settlement southward, villages, farms, outposts, reduced to ash and bone."

Silence fell. Hours before, they'd laughed over supper in the common room, delighting children with tales. Now, grim reality closed in like a wave of ice.

Rika sat between Arbor and Kumar on the central divan, her saddlebags nestled close. The room hummed with tension, Blair and Shandar lingered near the hearth, conspicuously apart. Whatever fragile alliance they'd forged that morning now hung splintered, brittle as ice.

But Rika's focus lay elsewhere.

She slipped the Star of Serenity over her head. Its weight settled against her chest, a ritual, a tether against unraveling.

Kumar's hand touched her forearm. "Is it wise? You should conserve your strength."

Her smile barely formed. "Routine keeps me sane. I just want to see Blaze."

She closed her eyes.

The rupture came quiet but violent. Her spirit tore free, the wild thrill of weightlessness replacing pain. Kumar's grip anchored her physical form as she slipped downward, through age-warped floorboards, into the stables.

Blaze shifted restlessly in his stall. Her presence brushed his flank, a whisper on the edge of sensation. He shivered, turned, snorted at nothing.

The groom paused, hand frozen mid-brush.

Rika drifted upward, past rafters and beams, through the inn's sloped roof. The grounds spread below, bathed in twilight gold.

Southeast, something shimmered. A distortion in the weave of the world, colors bending unnaturally.

She descended, drawn to the anomaly, her borrowed heart racing.

Three figures huddled around a campfire off Escap Road. One tended a horse. Two spoke in hushed tones.

Then, recognition. A pulse through her astral form like sunlight through cracked glass.

She passed through the shimmer.

"Merric?" The name escaped her.

The royal gamekeeper stirred his pot, teaching a young guard. He stiffened, as if hearing his name sung from the trees.

Kumar's voice entered her mind: Is he here?

Nearby, she replied, forgetting the Star carried her thoughts to shared ears. Let me reach him.

She placed both hands on Merric's head.

The flood came without warning, Queen Ellis's pale worry, King Vardon's measured weight, Sholin's piercing gaze. And beneath them all...

Fierce, undiluted love. For her.

It hit like flame across bare skin. She knelt midair, breathless, thoughts scattered.

Merric spun. "Rika?" he asked the darkness.

His guards exchanged glances, but Rika barely noticed.

She projected a vision: Red Lion walls, flickering hearth light. Her message tentative at first, his answer steady as stone.

"The Red Lion," he said, rising. "We'll come tonight. Baltan! Rasslow! Break camp, we move!"

Then something new, Merric pressed a hand over his heart. A gesture he'd never offered before.

Rika's spirit snapped back, folding inward like water into stone.

She gasped into her body. Kumar still held her arm, eyes searching.

"They're coming," she whispered, voice raw. "We must warn Bernard."

Kumar squeezed her hand. "I'll handle the innkeeper. Rest now." He guided her to a chair.

As she removed the Star, the door beside the hallway vanished. Panicked, she replaced it, the door reappeared. Once more she removed it, only silk remained.

"Blair," she called. "A hidden door. I see it only with the Star."

He ran his hands over the wall. "Nothing."

Shandar approached, muttering, "Stupid magic." Orange flame roiled around her hands. "I'll show you a door!" Green light blossomed from her fingertips, tracing a rectangle. The outline of a door glowed into view.

Arbor moved to open it, but Shandar caught his shoulder. "No, this needs magic."

"My lady," Arbor bowed his head, "you are too precious to risk. Merric arrives soon."

Their eyes met. Something unspoken passed between them. Shandar brushed his cheek. "Be safe, my friend."

Arbor knelt. "My lady honors me." He took an oil lamp and disappeared through the door.

Finrod cleared his throat. "You said Merric's name the moment you left us. Was he that close?"

"Yes." Rika described the distortion and the overwhelming wave of emotion upon touching him. "I failed to explore further."

"Perhaps he caused the distortion." Finrod's brow furrowed. "Have you seen such things before?"

"Never."

Finrod studied her. "He is much older than you. Is that... proper?"

Heat rose to her face. "Not like that. He saved my life, taught me courage, stood by me through disaster." She explained the paternal nature of their bond.

Finrod exchanged a glance with Blair before asking, "And his relation to your mother, Blair?"

Blair stiffened. "Ellis grew up beside him. He protected her as a child, introduced her to my father, remained her closest friend."

"Any other findings?" Blair asked Rika.

She blanched, realizing her oversight. "I'm sorry, I forgot to search further."

Blair gently lifted her chin. "We're safe until morning. Rest. Tomorrow, check the road ahead." He guided her toward the stairs.

After she left, Shandar and Finrod exchanged relieved smiles. A serving woman entered to light lamps, but Shandar waved her hand, every lamp ignited at once. The woman fled in terror.

"We must be gracious," Blair chided. "To them, this innkeeper's task is his pride."

Finrod raised his glass. "Spoken like a king."

Blair's smile tightened. "My mother taught me to remember what it feels like to be ordinary."

Shandar leaned against his chest. "A hug?" she teased. He stumbled over a chair, laughing despite himself.

Arbor returned, dust coating his clothes. "Escape route leads to an abandoned barn north of here."

A commotion at the stairway silenced them. Kumar entered with Merric and two guardsmen. Shandar slipped into shadows; Blair and Finrod remained seated. Merric knelt before Blair.

"My prince."

Blair introduced those present. "Rika is above," he added.

Merric presented the two young men. "Baltan Wain-wright and Rasslow Langdon, both made at the temple alongside Shandar."

Once seated, Merric delivered his report. "Queen Ellis sends her love. Sholin entrusted me with gifts, a diary for Rika, a scroll for Shandar that only she can read." He bowed toward Shandar's hiding place. "Mistress of Fire, I stand at your service with these two." His weathered face creased. "Fate plays games."

Shandar emerged, accepting graciously. "My mother spoke of you as the Queen's rock. Guide us and look after Rika."

Blair and Finrod nodded their agreement.

Merric knelt with his men and intoned the ancient oath of service. When it was done, Blair helped Rika, who had returned silently, to her feet. Together with Shandar, they welcomed their new companions.

Merric pressed a black velvet-bound book into Rika's hands. "The diary of the last Astral."

Her fingers trembled as she accepted it.

At dawn, they gathered in the common room, guards, elves in human guise, Merric, and Bernard. Shandar held the door for Blair and Rika, her eyes narrowing at their closeness.

Bernard introduced his wife Karen, who curtsied before Blair, then promptly fainted.

Rika knelt beside her. "It's all right, Karen. The past is forgiven." The innkeeper's wife rose shakily, fetched food, and they ate while Merric spoke of war, dark armies, fallen cities, refugees streaming toward Tiereny.

Bernard offered supplies. Reid, a local, volunteered to guide them to Wund's Mound.

"The path opens only to elven magic," Reid explained.

Rika revealed her Star. Reid grinned. "You'll need living elves. None seen in five hundred seasons."

Finrod removed his crystal. The air around the three elves shimmered as their true forms appeared, tall, graceful, otherworldly. Reid dropped to one knee, his companion fled.

The age of legends had returned to the Red Lion Inn.

Blair stared at his untouched meal, unease etched across his face. He leaned toward Rika. "Could you visit my mother? The pen in the bottom drawer of her desk, she'll recognize it."

Rika nodded. The magic ripped her free, wild, and unpracticed. Her spirit tumbled upward, tangled in memory-threads and emotional noise until a pulse of garden light steadied her. She surged toward the Queen's Garden, drawn by scent, Ka spice, lavender ink, sun-warmed parchment.

In Queen Ellis's study, the pen stirred.

Ellis reclined on her lounge, one hand holding a cup of Ka, the other clutching reports. Across from her, Glorin waited. He noticed first.

"Mother, look!"

A pen and parchment lifted from the desk, floating toward Ellis like memory seeking voice. They settled on an untouched corner where gravity seemed softened by sentiment.

Ellis's fingers brushed the pen she'd once gifted Blair. "It's from him," she whispered.

The pen whirled, inscribing words like smoke:

Rika Blair is well. Merric and his young ones with us. Just short of finding Dagmar. I'm in the room. Speak freely.

Ellis's voice broke. "The daughter I never had."

Across the miles, Rika's cheeks burned. The Queen's reply unfolded in waves:

"Tell Blair his family is well. We will raise a show of force but cannot hold the city. Our last stand will be in Tiereny." Her voice strengthened. "Blair must save us, the gods chose him."

Then softer: "Rika... love him as I do. He is yours always. I knew when I first saw you. Believe in love. Let it protect you both."

The pen rose once more:

We have the Mistress of Fire! As my Queen wishes, so shall it be done, mother. Safe Journey.

The pen dropped to the floor.

Glorin retrieved it. "Rika? The one who slapped Saad? She is to be my sister?"

Ellis didn't answer. Her shoulders slumped, voice low and monotone. "If nature is truly in balance, and we survive the coming storm... Orders will wait. Mid-morning. I must think."

Glorin bowed and left.

Ellis touched the parchment once more. She smiled, not as Queen, but as something older, something softer. She'd heard her name spoken not in court, but from the girl who now carried their fate.

CHAPTER 15

THE RED LION UNDER ATTACK

The inn shuddered. A thunderous boom sent them all staggering as dust and plaster rained from the ceiling.

Arbor and Kumar bolted for the stairway. Finrod whistled sharply, halting Kumar with a look that conveyed volumes between the elven warriors.

Rika closed her eyes and slipped free of her body, her spirit descending the stairs like mist.

Hell had erupted below. The kitchen's back wall had been blown apart, leaving a jagged hole through which Northmen poured like ants from a broken hill. The kitchen itself blazed, flames licking up cabinets and across ceiling beams. Between the breach and the hearth, nothing remained but splinters and bodies. Two patrons and a serving girl lay twisted in unnatural stillness, blood pooling beneath them.

Near the stage, a gray-haired man with a wooden cane, the wordsmith who had been telling children's tales earlier, herded terrified children behind him. Northmen advanced through the common room, axes and swords dripping red.

Rika spotted Shandar and Baltan trapped in their booth. Rasslow lunged into view, wielding a ceramic pitcher against the first Northman to reach them. The improvised weapon connected with a sickening crack against the raider's temple. As the man crumpled, Rasslow snatched his fallen sword.

A streak of orange light cut through the air, a fireball hurled across the room. It passed through Rika's ethereal form, leaving a sensation like ice and fire mingled. She bit back a cry no one would hear. The fireball struck the wall behind Shandar's booth with a concussive blast that hurled both Shandar and Baltan across the floor.

Rika spun toward the source of the magic. A man stood framed in the breach of medium height with dark hair and a flat face. Slanted eyes glinted above his beard, from which hung three braids interwoven with runes that pulsed with malevolent light. His fingers traced another spell pattern in the air.

Movement caught Rika's attention as Arbor reaching the bottom stair. Time to go. She snapped back to her body with a gasp.

"Northmen," she reported, her voice clipped as she gripped the armrests to stop her hands from shaking. "They've blown through the back wall by the kitchen. The wordsmith is protecting children on the stage. A mage with them throwing fireballs. Shandar and Baltan are down. They're killing everyone." Her nostrils flared with each rapid breath.

Blair buckled on his sword belt with practiced efficiency. Finrod returned from arming Kumar with a bow and quiver. Blair absorbed her report, his face hardening into the mask of command.

"Rika, gather everyone's bags from the rooms that keep you safely away from the fighting." His tone brooked no argument. "Finrod, you and Kumar secure this stairway. I'll get our people back up here, then we take the hidden passage to the farm."

He drew Comet, the blade gleaming with an inner light. As he passed Kumar, he added, "See if we can bring horses through the tunnel. If not, determine if we can get them up these stairs. Be cautious."

Kumar bowed and vanished down the hidden corridor. Blair took the stairs three at a time, plunging into chaos.

Six paces from the bottom stair, Shandar lay motionless on the floor. Baltan knelt beside her, desperately trying to revive her. Blair's heart stopped.

We can't be doomed already. I promised to keep her safe.

Then her smallest finger twitched, and breath returned to his lungs.

The common room had become a battlefield. Arbor and Rasslow fought back-to-back against four Northmen, while overturned tables formed a makeshift barricade behind which survivors huddled. To his right, the remaining patrons wielded broken table legs, desperately fending off attackers trying to climb over their barrier. Left, near the stage, the wordsmith jabbed his cane at a Northman advancing on the children.

Behind it all stood the mage, hands weaving a pattern of destruction.

A fireball screamed toward Blair. He dove left, rolling across sticky floorboards. His hand closed around a fallen stool's leg, and he hurled it at the Northman, threatening the wordsmith. The distraction was enough. The old man thrust his cane through his attacker's eye socket with surprising strength, then wrenched the sword from lifeless fingers.

The wordsmith flashed a grateful smile that Blair never saw. He was already dodging another fireball, feeling its heat singe his hair.

Landing in a crouch, Blair swept the legs from one of Arbor's opponents. Above him, Comet moved of its own accord, splitting an incoming fireball into harmless sparks that rained down around them.

The mage changed tactics, launching two fireballs in rapid succession along different paths. Blair ducked beneath both, but the second struck the hearth's chimney. The impact rang out like a massive bell, showering the room with brick dust and embers.

Blair charged. Three strides brought him to a table. He vaulted across it, tucked into a roll, and came up with Comet already leaving his hand. The sword spun through the air, its blade catching firelight as it turned. With a wet thud, it embedded itself in the mage's chest, pinning him to the wall.

No time for relief. Blair sprinted to retrieve his sword as three more Northmen poured through the breach, their eyes fixing on the children.

Blair yanked at Comet, but the blade had sunk deep into the wall. He glanced over his shoulder and saw Shandar sitting up, supported by Baltan.

"Shandar!" he shouted, cupping his hands around his mouth. "The children!"

She heard. Her head snapped toward the stage where the wordsmith, now armed with a sword, fought desperately against overwhelming odds. Three Northmen closed in from different angles. The old man's sword arm was tiring, his swings growing wild.

Shandar struggled to her feet with Baltan's help. Her knees buckled, then steadied. She pushed Baltan back and thrust her arm forward.

A thin rope of fire, no thicker than a bowstring but burning white-hot, lanced from her fingertips. It pierced the first Northman through his back and continued through the second's midsection. Both collapsed like puppets with cut strings.

The wordsmith stumbled and fell. The third Northman leapt forward, sword raised for a killing blow.

"NO!" Shandar's voice cracked like thunder.

A pulse of white light erupted from her mouth, crossing the distance instantaneously. When it touched the Northman, he simply... disintegrated. A small puff of dust where a killer had stood.

Shandar collapsed to her knees, spent. The magical exertion after her injury had drained her completely. Baltan scooped her up over his shoulder and carried her toward the stairs, away from the remaining danger.

Blair braced his boot against the wall and wrenched Comet free. He peered through the breach, no reinforcements visible. Turning back, he assessed what remained of the battle.

Rasslow and Arbor had pushed their opponents back but weren't finishing them. Three patrons remained trapped against the front wall, facing three Northmen.

Six enemies left. Three near the hearth, three by the door. Forty paces separating them.

Blair decided and sprinted toward the trapped patrons. Two strides in, a Northman's blade slashed across Rasslow's thigh. The man went down with a cry.

Blair changed direction, leaping onto a table and launching himself toward Rasslow's attacker. Comet swept in a backhand arc, striking the Northman with such force it knocked him into his companion. The third stepped back, but Arbor was faster, driving his blade through the man's chest. In one fluid motion, the elf spun and buried his dagger in the off-balance raider's neck.

Blair finished the last with a backward strike over his head as he completed his roll. He glanced at Rasslow. Arbor was already tying off the wound with a belt.

The three Northmen by the door remained. Blair sheathed Comet and ran six strides toward them. He leapt, caught the carved lion's head beside the door, and used it to change direction mid-air. His boot connected with the first Northman's chest, sending him crashing into his companion.

The third raider was quicker. As his comrades fell, he lunged over them, driving his sword into a patron's stomach. The man's eyes widened in shock as life drained from them.

Before the Northman could free his blade, the second patron smashed a table leg across his skull.

The last raider staggered to his feet. The surviving patron rushed forward, weapon raised for a killing blow.

"Hold!" Blair's command cut through the chaos. "I need him for information. Tie him up. I'll return shortly."

Both men froze, then bowed their heads. "Yes, Your Highness."

Blair turned and took the stairs two at a time, returning to check on the others. Anxiety and dread followed him like a shadow, but beneath them, an icy determination was forming. Their enemies had found them once. They wouldn't get a second chance.

Kumar brushed past Blair on the stairs, his normally stoic, elven face alight with relief. "Yes, they live," he said, continuing down without breaking stride.

Blair paused, one foot on the next step. "Yes, what?" But Kumar was already gone. Dread churning in his gut, Blair took the remaining stairs two at a time.

The scene that greeted him wasn't what he expected. Finrod and Merric sat in armchairs wearing the foolish grins of men who've cheated death. Baltan perched on the divan, hands twisting in his lap, head tilting nervously as his eyes darted toward the privy door. Despite the absence of the women, relief hung in the air like a physical presence.

From the open privy came the unmistakable sounds of retching, followed by soft, soothing murmurs. Female voices. Alive!

As Blair approached Baltan, the young guardsman slid to his knees, head bowed. "Forgive me, my lord. I did not protect..."

Blair gripped his shoulders and hauled him to his feet, locking eyes with him. "You saved all of Monde and kept her alive. By doing so, you've given us a chance to stop this madness." His voice dropped, steady and certain. "I won't forgive you for saving us all, Baltan. Instead, I'll commend you for a job well done. Be at peace we live today. Tomorrow, we fight again."

Blair squeezed the guardsman's shoulders and turned toward Merric, aware of Baltan's darting glances and the hard swallow that worked his throat.

"Spare any of that?" Blair nodded at Merric's glass.

Without a word, Merric handed it over. Blair drained the brandy in one burning swallow. Suddenly, his body betrayed him as violent tremors racked his frame, teeth chattering, muscles spasming. Merric guided him into the vacated chair where Blair sat, eyes closed, unable to control the shaking.

"What's happening to me?" he managed through clenched teeth. "I've never..."

"Better after than before or during," Finrod replied, his scholarly tone softening with rare compassion. "You're releasing the fear you held at bay. Think of it as shaking off the trauma. The danger passed, you relaxed, and it hit you all at once." The elven lord leaned forward, his smile tinged with wonder. "You should feel weakness once the fear fully leaves your system."

"Rika watched it all," Merric added quietly. "From the ceiling. She told us what was happening. Had Baltan fetch Shandar when she regained consciousness." He hesitated. "She's... upset about witnessing the carnage. And you being its star."

Blair's hands steadied enough to pour more brandy. "She'll have to see worse before we're done. That was a squad with a mage-warrior as leader." He sipped, the liquid warming paths through his chilled core. "Was it luck they found us, or are we being tracked? That's the third time I've faced Northmen, now with magic added." His voice hardened. "Chance grows thin."

He called to Baltan, who hovered near the door. "Get everyone up here. We need to talk." As Baltan turned to leave, Blair added, "And see if we can bring the horses through that hole in the back wall. We'll need them up here, ready to move."

Baltan nodded sharply and disappeared down the stairs, relief at having a purpose clear in his quickened step.

The privy door opened. Rika appeared, eyes downcast, and stood before them. "Shandar is... rejuvenating. She'll join us shortly." When she met Blair's gaze, he saw the horror of what she'd seen warring with determination not to show weakness.

Blair tried projecting hope toward her, though he felt none himself. He shifted uncomfortably, aware of his own hypocrisy. There will be a next day. And a day after that. Whether they'd live to see them was another matter entirely.

Something in his silent message reached her. Rika's spine straightened, her shoulders squared.

The door opened again, and Shandar entered. Blair was on his feet instantly, crossing to her in three long strides. He pulled her into a fierce embrace, his lips close to her ear.

"Never let it get easier," he whispered. "Remember the price paid. You saved those children." His breath caught, and he forced himself to inhale deeply, steadying his voice. "You saved them all."

Holding her at arm's length, he offered a smile that spoke of shared burdens and mutual strength. He tucked her arm through his, leading her to the others. Finrod and Merric rose in respect, or perhaps in awe of what she'd done. Shandar squeezed Rika's hand as she passed, a silent acknowledgment between women who'd seen too much. She took the vacant chair with preternatural calm.

Arbor appeared at the top of the stairs, supporting Rasslow, who hobbled toward the divan, blood darkening his trouser leg. Blair helped lift Rasslow's injured limb, examining the wound with practiced eyes.

Kumar approached, his movements fluid despite the recent battle. "The horses can be brought through from the back. We found the stableman hiding in the farthest stall." His lip curled in disdain. "Baltan has him helping with the fire, but he'll join us shortly."

Kumar returned to the liquor table where Arbor joined him. Baltan entered, starting at a run, then slowing awkwardly as all eyes turned to him. He moved to support Rasslow's leg while Blair completed his examination.

"He almost missed you," Blair said with a grim smile. "We'll stitch and bandage it. Be gentle, don't tear the stitches. If blood soaks through, speak up at once. It'll hurt, but you're not out of commission. Keep it clean." He rose to retrieve needle and thread from his saddlebag.

Baltan followed, taking the medical kit. "My job," he said simply. Blair nodded, grateful for the small normalcy of hierarchy in their chaotic world.

Taking a position beside Rika, Blair faced the group. How do I fall into this shite? he thought, then pushed aside the self-pity. Lives depended on him.

"We'll bring the horses up here and each lead our own to the farm," he said, scrubbing a hand over his face. "Then ride northeast cross-country, directly to Wund Mound. We're being hunted, whether by luck or design doesn't matter. We need Dagmar. One task at a time." He looked around the room. "Ideas?"

Merric leaned forward. "We get the people downstairs to tell everyone we rode west. We can ensure their cooperation by putting out their fire."

Shandar stirred, her trance-like calm breaking. "I can end it. I'll tell the fire to stop." She stood, suddenly decisive. "Arbor, will you come with me?"

Arbor was at her side instantly, escorting her downstairs.

Blair offered his chair to Rika, but she pushed him down instead, standing protectively at his shoulder. Finrod's eyebrows rose as he glanced between Arbor's swift response to Shandar and Rika's protective stance beside Blair. Merric leaned back, silent laughter playing across his features.

Baltan and Rasslow approached, field kit returned, standing stiffly side by side. Their uncertain posture spoke volumes. Blair caught the telltale twitch of Rasslow's shoulders, the instinct to salute warring with their informal surroundings.

"You're Royal Guardsmen," Blair said, understanding dawning. "Wondering about protocol. We don't stand on ceremony here, no ranks, no salutes. Do what's needed or what you're asked. For now, get the horses through the back wall, saddled and packed. We move out when the fire's extinguished and Shandar returns."

Both men saluted, caught themselves, then turned and left.

Rika approached Merric, taking his hand to guide him from his seat, which she claimed. Merric shook his head, pointing to her neck. Rika's fingers found the Star of Serenity hanging there. She removed it, tucking it into her pouch before closing her eyes, her face relaxing as she prepared for astral projection. Merric joined Kumar at the liquor table, filling a fresh glass.

"Blair asked if you've done your scan. Reid has returned; we leave shortly." Baltan's voice startled Rika from her contemplation at the bar.

She sighed, offering a smile that didn't reach her eyes. "Let me finish my Ka first." She sipped the strong tea, a clear dismissal.

The moment he turned away, she slipped from her body, her astral form following him. She hadn't meant to be cold, but the strain of recent events had frayed her patience.

Baltan returned to his own cup at the damaged counter, shoulders slumped. Karen approached from behind the bar, her movements listless, face slack with shock. The innkeeper's wife, who had once been so vibrant, now moved like a sleepwalker.

"Thanks again for helping with the bodies," she said, fingers clenching and unclenching. "Maybe something can be salvaged." Her eyes flicked to his uniform, then away. "You call him Blair, not Prince or Your Majesty. You wear the royal insignia. How can you disrespect him so?"

Baltan drained his Ka, squaring his shoulders. He rubbed his chest absently, voice flattening as he clutched a splintered piece of wood a memento from the destroyed booth.

"His Royal Majesty, Prince Blair Willow, carries the weight of the land on his shoulders. His decisions guide our quest." Something hardened in Baltan's expression. "He hates the honorifics. We call him Blair to avoid distracting him from what matters." A pause. "Besides, I was speaking to his favorite confidant and familiar. That's how she thinks of him."

I'm his favorite? The thought caught Rika by surprise.

Baltan departed without another word. Karen retreated to the kitchen, mechanical in her movements.

Rika's consciousness snapped back to her body. She blinked, orienting herself, then rose and made her way upstairs.

The scene before her was deceptively ordinary preparations for departure, as they'd done countless mornings. Yet they stood in the royal apartments of the damaged Red Lion Inn, before a secret door leading to some unknown farm. Merric and Finrod supervised as Arbor and Kumar readied the supply horses. Blair stood apart, the medallion in his palm, eyes unfocused as he planned their next move. Baltan, Rasslow, and Shandar loaded their mounts, their banter belying the danger they faced. Karen and Bernard moved among them, collecting cups, farewell gifts clutched in nerveless fingers. The payment Merric had pressed upon them offered little comfort to those who'd lost everything. Reid leaned against his horse, waiting with the patient stillness of a seasoned scout.

Rika approached Blair directly.

"Blair." She waited for his focus to return, noting the shadows beneath his eyes, the tension in his jaw. "Two bands will reach here by late afternoon, the third by nightfall. An enormous force of those monsters approaches along the king's road." She swallowed. "This is separate from what's attacking Eastport. I don't know how they're moving so quickly, only that they are."

She turned, catching Karen and Bernard's attention.

"You must leave with us," she said, her voice allowing no argument. "Gather what you need. We'll prepare your horses. Tell the others everyone must go. Now. There's no time."

The innkeepers exchanged a glance, then hurried to comply.

Approaching Shandar, she said, "Bal, Ras, would you saddle the innkeepers' horses? They're coming with us. Thank you."

The guardsmen bowed their heads in unison before leaving.

Shandar's lips quirked. "Ordering my friends around? Your head is growing."

Rika felt a spark of something lighten her chest. Not quite humor, but close. Her eyes brightened.

"I have an idea. Are you willing to try something completely impossible?"

Shandar's eyes widened, a genuine smile spreading across her face. "What do you have in mind?"

"We'll need to work together, share a vision," Rika said, suddenly serious. "It might lead to knowing each other more deeply, good and bad. Are you certain you want to open yourself to me that way?"

Shandar's answer came without hesitation. "My sister, it will be my honor to know you so well. An unexpected gift." She leaned closer, anticipation replacing exhaustion. "What are we planning to do?"

"You remember moving Blair from the campfire to our sides?" Rika said, her voice barely above a whisper. "That means you can move anyone to a place, you know." She leaned closer, her evergreen eyes bright with possibility. "If I give you the vision of the location, you'll know it and be able to move them there. I want you to transport Karen and Bernard and their horses to Karen's family farm."

She bit her lip and covered her mouth, waiting.

Shandar's head jerked back as if slapped. "You're mad." She slashed her hand through the air. "Two adults and their horses across half the realm? To a place I've never seen?" She spun around. "Finrod! Do you hear this lunatic? Tell her it's impossible!"

Finrod approached, his elvish features unexpectedly visible without his crystal disguise. Shandar startled at his true visage: the angular cheekbones, the pointed ears, the otherworldly grace momentarily thrown off her argument.

Finrod chuckled and placed a steadying arm around her shoulders. "What has distressed you so, Mistress?"

"She thinks I can move two horses and riders across half the land to a place I've never laid eyes on." Shandar's voice pitched higher. "And she wants to meld minds with me to share all my thoughts. It can't be done." She tucked a strand of hair behind her ear, a nervous habit betraying her uncertainty.

Finrod studied Rika for a long moment, those ancient eyes taking measure of her conviction. Then he turned to Shandar, hands gentle but firm on her shoulders.

"She is your sister in all ways that matter," he said, his voice soft but carrying the weight of centuries. "Trust Rika as you would trust yourself. She understands magic not as rules to be followed, but as truth to be shaped." His eyes held Shandar's. "Under harrowing circumstances, she has gleaned what scholars spend lifetimes seeking. I trust her with my life and my destiny." He stepped back and bowed. "She is remarkable in her own right. She only pales next to you, Mistress of Fire."

He straightened, adding, "If it helps, when the great castles were built, master mages floated stone blocks from quarry to construction site. When you meld together, embrace the differences between you." His eyes twinkled with mischief. "Oh, and try not to crack the land in half. You are quite capable of that." He turned and walked back to his horse.

Shandar stood frozen, mouth ajar. "Why do they always caution me like that?" she muttered. "I don't just unleash magic without thinking." She stared at the ground, mind racing. "They could simply come with us... No, that wouldn't be good for Rika."

She exhaled sharply. "Fine. When we meld, who leads?"

"I don't know," Rika admitted. "I've never done this. But I know it will work." She moved closer, her confidence softening. "I'll leave my body and float into yours, show you where, then you move them. Simple."

Seeing Shandar's doubt, she continued, "Distance isn't the problem. It's just here to there with nothing in between. Weight doesn't matter because it's all in your mind. You're just changing the picture's background." She swallowed. "All because you will it to happen. Understand?" Her voice lifted with a tremor of hope.

Shandar's eyes unfocused as she reasoned through it. "Simple really. Magic is simple; the power of the user differs." Her brow furrowed. "Power is the lure, the true flaw. Power corrupts absolutely..." She stiffened. "Where did that come from? Am I corrupt because of my power?" The muscles around her mouth tightened as she covered it with her hand.

A presence invaded her consciousness not in words, but in pure thought: I have come, sister.

Shandar's defenses flared instinctively. She thrust the presence out with such force that Rika collapsed, clutching her head, face contorted in pain.

"Rika, was that you?" Shandar's hands shot forward, palms out.

"I melded with you," Rika gasped, fingers tangled in her hair, "and then my head exploded." She looked up, eyes watering. "Was that you?"

Shandar paled, a haunted look crossing her face. She tried to speak, but her voice cracked. After a deep, shuddering breath, she closed her eyes. "Yes. But I'll know now."

The presence returned, tentative this time: I have come, sister.

Rika, is that you? Shandar thought back.

I've melded with you and can show you where. Ready?

As I'll ever be. Let's do it.

Picture them on their horses. Look at them, take them in. Now come with me...

Shandar's vision dimmed, then sharpened with startling clarity. She stood beneath a massive oak tree, sunlight filtering through its ancient branches. Emotions not her own flooded her consciousness, the flutter of a first kiss, the crimson blush that followed, the ache of young heartbreak.

Rika, I'm sorry for the loss you feel.

This place holds powerful emotions for me. The meld follows the strongest feelings. That's why we're experiencing my first kiss. I was ten. I got past it. A hesitation. What about you? When was your first kiss?

Their shared consciousness darkened. A scruffy face loomed close, breath reeking of mead, pork, and garlic as wet lips slobbered against Shandar's mouth. The memory carried the terror of a young girl as her mother burst in, dragging the man from her bedroom. Violation and fear pulsed through both women, and Shandar's body shuddered physically.

Shandar, that was horrible. How do you not think of it constantly?

I lock it away. The thought came flat, final.

Back to why we're here, Rika redirected gently. Look around, feel this glade. Now picture Karen and Bernard on horseback beside this tree.

Shandar concentrated, and suddenly they both saw it Karen and Bernard materializing on horseback, blinking in confusion as they found themselves in a sun-dappled clearing, their horses pawing at lush grass.

But Rika noticed two problems. A corner section of the Red Lion's barn had also appeared, tilting before crashing down. A startled horse burst free, eyes wild, and galloped away with tail held high. Behind the riders sat the stable cart, a curious cat peering over its edge.

Karen waved, then turned at the crash. She quickly dismounted to retrieve the bewildered cat. The distant figures of their companions came into focus as Shandar felt a sudden hollowness wash through her.

Rika broke the meld and stumbled to her feet. She ran to Shandar, embracing her fiercely. "You're magnificent," she whispered, her breath warm against Shandar's ear. "I love you, sister." She pulled back slightly. "The power that flowed through me. I've felt nothing like it. Focus was the issue, I think. Just the subjects, not the entire picture."

"You're the one who said, 'get the picture,'" Shandar replied with a weak smile. "I got the picture."

She hugged Rika tighter, a profound sense of belonging washing over her. "I love you, Rika," she whispered back, tilting her head to blink away tears.

"All is well, ladies?" Blair approached, his voice gentle but urgent. "The innkeepers are gone, though the barn..." He glanced between them, clearly uncertain how to address the intensity of their embrace. "I wish I could give you time to celebrate this remarkable feat, but we must leave to stay ahead of our pursuers."

They reluctantly separated, though their hands remained clasped as they bowed to the prince. The touch lingered as they finally parted to retrieve their horses, joining the others as the group set off through the hidden passage toward the Mound.

CHAPTER 16

THE BARGAIN

The waarzeggerij hung suspended in the air, its ornate frame of intertwined branches casting faint shadows across Vardon's study. Runes etched into its glass surface flickered as it displayed an aerial view of Eastport. King Vardon leaned forward at his desk, the lines in his face deepening as he studied the image.

"Three hundred strides maximum for flaming arrow accuracy," Vardon said, tracing his finger along the city's outer defenses. "If we cover the oil with grass, they won't see it until they're standing in it."

Sholin sat in one of the two cushioned chairs facing the magical device, his silence more condemning than any rebuke. The other chair remained empty. Ellis was somewhere in the castle, managing the latest crisis spawned by thirty thousand refugees crammed into a city built for ten thousand.

Vardon refused to meet his advisor's eyes. "Twelve thousand soldiers," he continued, voice growing firmer as if conviction alone could alter their fate. He rubbed at his brow, the gesture betraying his exhaustion. "Two flanking forces to break apart their advance before they reach the walls. It's a good plan." His voice faltered on the last word. "We can win."

The silence stretched between them.

"Magic," Sholin finally said, his deep frown revealing his thinning patience. "That's what can't be planned for. An escape route is necessary, my king. You must decide."

Vardon's shoulders slumped. For a king to plan retreat was to admit defeat before the battle began. Yet the reports from fallen cities left little room for pride.

"Build the floating bridge across the river," he hissed, the words tasting like ash. "Take down the wall in the back northwest corner, large enough for two wagons." A bitter smile touched his lips. "Having the castle along the river was supposed to be a defensive advantage. Let's hope we don't need to discover otherwise."

The door opened as servants entered with the evening meal, the mundane ritual momentarily breaking the tension. Ellis glided in behind them, her composure immaculate despite the chaos enveloping their kingdom. The servants arranged her table and meal with practiced efficiency. She crossed her legs and dismissed them with a graceful wave, offering Vardon a smile that didn't quite reach her eyes.

"My King, have you made your decision?" she asked. "I need to keep these people occupied. We have a tinderbox out there. Any spark could ignite a conflagration worse than the Horde itself." Her voice softened. "Idle hands, mischief they make."

Vardon looked up from his barely touched plate. Even now, with doom approaching their gates, her beauty struck him anew. Even if I die, he thought, I have the memory of you beside me.

"Floating bridge and back wall, enough for two wagons," he confirmed. "I just told Sho. The shipping will stop, so you'll need a temporary dock north of the bridge."

As he spoke, the waarzeggerij's image shifted, pulling back to show a greater expanse of territory. Vardon's words died in his throat. "They're coming from the north. How did they get there already?"

All three leaned forward, transfixed by the horror unfolding before them.

North of Eastport, a dark mass materialized like black sand pouring from an invisible hand. The waarzeggerij showed it expanding outward, twenty-five hundred strides from the wall, fifteen hundred from Out Town, that ramshackle collection of dwellings and shops that had grown beyond Eastport's protection. The eastern edge of the mass bled toward the King's Road, forming a spearhead that widened as it advanced toward the city. Thin smoke rose in its wake.

Sholin flicked his fingers apart. The view zoomed closer, revealing individual creatures reaching Out Town's edge. Tall and muscular, their heads were nothing but skulls with thin, protruding snouts filled with needle-sharp teeth. Each carried a halberd combining spear point, axe blade, and hook.

The creatures moved in eerie unison down the main street. When the column's width reached the first buildings, their blades ignited with pale green fire. They didn't slow, didn't stop. They simply walked through everything in their path, their enchanted weapons slicing through wood, stone, and metal, leaving only burning ruins behind.

"At least there are no people running," Sholin whispered. "No one dying. They heeded your warning."

The waarzeggerij showed Eastport's wall two strides thick, not quite circular, with three gates and the seaport. Thirty strides of open ground separated it from Out Town's nearest structures. The Horde marched straight down Adanna Road toward the North Gate.

As the lead creature passed the last building, arrows suddenly pierced it from above. Twenty guardsmen and their commander, positioned atop the North Gate, fought to defend their city.

"No," Sholin breathed. "Not Warren. Fool!"

When the first creatures reached the wall and gate, they swung their glowing halberds against it, only to be met with unexpected resistance. Silver sparks showered down where each strike hit an invisible barrier. Oil poured from the battlements, igniting in a wall of flame that consumed dozens of the monstrosities.

But there were always more. Then, abruptly, the Horde halted. No more advances, no more swings of their terrible weapons. Complete stillness.

"Run, you fools," Vardon whispered, knuckles white as he gripped the edge of his desk.

"Is that a magical barrier?" he asked, a flicker of hope in his voice. "Where did it come from? Do we have defenses like that?"

"No," Sholin replied, distracted. "I'd forgotten Eastport's ancient barrier. It must date back thousands of seasons. Such magic was lost when the throne was established here."

In the distance, behind the motionless Horde, a small group approached. As they drew nearer, a murmur seemed to travel through the ranks of creatures, which parted like a dark sea before them.

Dust swirled around the newcomers' feet, creating a hazy aura. Their leader walked with such a commanding presence that the creatures continued stepping aside, forming a clear path. Sholin brought his hands together, then spread them wide, bringing the seven figures into sharp focus.

"Six warrior mages," he said, voice tight with dread, "and..."

His words faltered as he stared at the monstrous figure towering above the others. Unlike anything in nature, it had a muscular head with a bony framework, a broad snout with flaring nostrils, and prominent upward-curving horns. Its massive body stood upright on powerful legs, metallic skin gleaming in the sunlight, with small flaps of burned flesh scattered across its surface. In its hands, it carried a hammer whose head alone was the size of a calf.

"By all the gods," Sholin whispered. "What is that?"

The monster knelt before the gate. Its lips moved, and pale green smoke poured from its horns, reaching out to envelop each warrior mage. The smoke twisted into ropes, binding them to the creature, each cord attached to the back of their heads.

Rising to its full height, the monster approached the gate. Arrows bounced harmlessly off its metallic frame. It dropped the hammer head behind itself, the misty cords descending from its own head, running down its body to connect with the weapon seven braided strands in all.

"Linking all their power to one device," Sholin said in horrified awe. "That's unheard of." Beneath his breath, he added, "Please Lashnar, protect those people."

The monster took the hammer's handle over its shoulder. With knees bent, it lifted the massive head from the ground, then in one fluid motion, stepped forward and slammed it against the gate's magical barrier.

The braided cords shimmered with an eerie green light that matched the hammer's growing glow. The surrounding air crackled with energy, the green illumination intensifying until it painted everything in its sickly hue.

A concussive shock blasted backward, knocking over swaths of creatures behind the monster, including the warrior mages. The impact severed their connecting cords, but the green energy had already transferred to the gate, which still stood defiantly.

The twenty guards, somehow unaffected by the blast, hurled rocks from the wall's top. The projectiles bounced harmlessly off the monster's hide. It leaned forward, head tilted as if listening to something no one else could hear. Then it knelt, reaching out to grasp something invisible.

"It's sensing the magical vein powering the gate," Sholin whispered, his face ashen.

The monster squeezed.

The gate and a three-stride section of wall exploded inward with such force that it carved a channel four hundred strides deep, all the way to the steward's residence. The guardsmen vanished in the blast, their bodies obliterated. The Horde surged through the breach, their green-fire blades slashing through everything in their path, leaving only flames in their wake.

Sholin waved his hand sharply. The waarzeggerij went dark, its runes reappearing as it drifted to a corner of the room.

"As soon as that bridge is built, we must evacuate everyone," he said, his voice unsteady. "We cannot stand against that. I don't have the magic to combat it." He rose from his chair, shoulders bent as if bearing an invisible weight. "I must confer with Tartus immediately. You need to direct everyone to Tiereny. We'll make our stand there and pray Blair saves us."

The disturbance in his usually composed voice was more terrifying than any words. With a brief bow, he excused himself and left the study.

Ellis sat frozen, one fist pressed against her mouth, eyes wide with horror. When Vardon turned to her, she spoke without being asked, her voice barely above a whisper.

"I'll have the project doubled, tripled whatever it takes to complete it as quickly as possible." She swallowed hard. "You must warn Tiereny of what's coming, both people and destruction." Her voice broke. "May your ancestors give us the time we need."

She turned away, shielding her face with one trembling hand.

Vardon's head fell into his hands as the truth crashed down upon him like the monster's hammer. There would be no victory, no clever strategy to save his people. His kingdom was already lost.

The sun had vanished, leaving only a crimson smear across the western sky where a distant cloud caught the day's final breath. Sholin paced the dock, fingers combing through his white hair, hands clenching into fists, then releasing, his movements betraying the anxiety his composed face would not. He paused, listening intently to the lap of water against the pilings.

Waiting always made it worse.

Dockworkers lit oil lamps along the wharf, their flames pushing back the natural darkness with artificial twilight. Sholin watched them while monitoring the half-finished bridge spanning the river, its center section still open for river traffic. The urgent message from this Captain Quick troubled him. In his thousand years of life, Sholin had learned that coincidence was far rarer than design, especially with monsters bearing down on their kingdom.

The dockworkers cast furtive glances his way. They performed their duties with deliberate focus, yet each man found reason to study the royal wizard when they thought he wasn't looking.

Sholin turned back toward the river and froze. A massive ship had somehow berthed without a sound, without his notice. The hair on the back of his neck bristled.

"Krevaan staht," he whispered, the strength spell flowing through his limbs as he focused on the gangplank being lowered from the vessel.

A compact figure of surprising girth descended and strode directly toward him. At ten paces, the stranger passed under a torch, and the light revealed his full appearance. Shock rooted Sholin in place. Three more steps passed before he shook his head clear.

"Caldin Hardwfik," Sholin said, disbelief softening his voice. "Captain Quick. You've hardly aged a day." He shook his head slowly, glancing around to see if others saw this impossibility. Strangely, the dockworkers had vanished.

"That's because you're an old wizard," Caldin replied, studying Sholin's slender frame. "Look at you, all skin and white hair."

The torchlight illuminated Sholin's unmarked face, his pure white hair slicked back and cut sharply at the neck. His floor-length black robe rippled in the breeze, its quarter moon and solitary star embroidered in silver thread catching the lamplight.

"You people don't age well," Caldin added with a chuckle that sounded like gravel tumbling across wooden boards.

"The reason you don't change," Sholin replied, offering a thin smile, "is that you're so ugly to begin with. The gods must have some sympathy."

Caldin's laughter deepened. "The gods forgot about us before either of us were born. If they had any sympathy, they'd have made you a woman. At least then you'd have been manageable."

"You truly know nothing about women, do you?" Sholin tugged at his ear, eyes narrowing. "You've hidden too long underground. Why are you here, Caldin? Have you come to fight?"

The dwarf's expression hardened. "For those monsters, you need catapults and archers. One-on-one fighting against those beasts is suicide. There are only three of us dwarves here." He stepped closer, lowering his voice. "We want to slow them down. Teach them this won't be easy. My holds are filled with spark powder. We can create a matrix for a firestorm to delay their advance. It won't stop them, but it should buy you another day to evacuate. What do you think?"

Sholin tapped his index finger against his lip, brows furrowing. "After five hundred seasons, it's peculiar to see you now. Didn't your people abandon us to our fate?"

"We believe in balance," Caldin said simply. "The balance has changed. We're here to right it."

Sholin spun abruptly and strode away, then stopped and turned back. "Come," he said firmly. "Meet the King and Queen. Tell them your plan." His lips curved into the ghost of a smile. "I'm certain Ellis will hug you."

He turned toward the castle looming above the river-front, not waiting to see if the dwarf followed.

Queen Ellis sat at the table in her office, now transformed into the kingdom's command center, surrounded by maps and evacuation orders. She smoothed a wrinkle from her royal blue evening gown, one of many beautiful things she would never see again after they fled. Someone had spent hours crafting it; it deserved to be worn one last time.

She tried to focus on the reports before her, but her mind drifted as she watched Vardon stretched out on her lounge, drinking wine and reading dispatches. Beautiful, considerate, and impossibly stubborn, her husband had always been all three.

The door opened without a knock. Sholin entered, followed by a stocky, hairy figure with an enormous bulbous nose. Ellis stood up reflexively, eyes widening. She rubbed them, looked again, then pointed and exclaimed, "Dwarf!"

Vardon's wineglass slipped from his fingers, shattering against the floor. Diplomatic training reasserted itself, and he executed a slight bow, head only.

Sholin stepped between them. "Queen Ellis White-Willow, King Vardon Willow, may I present Caldin Hardwfik, King of the Dwarves, protector of the seal."

"A pleasure," Vardon said, recovering quickly. "I'm Vardon, and this is my wife, Ellis." He approached the dwarf, and they exchanged a forearm grip, though Caldin's attention remained fixed on Ellis.

"She has that effect on people," Vardon said dryly. "Ellis, come meet King Caldin." He extended his hand, and Ellis glided to his side, executing a full curtsy before reaching for the dwarf's arm.

Caldin took her hand in his massive one. "You needn't have dressed up for my arrival, though how you knew I was coming would be a fascinating tale." He kissed her hand with surprising gentleness, revealing clean, white teeth as he smiled.

"You're too kind, Your Majesty," Ellis replied, her posture straightening as curiosity brightened her eyes. "Dwarves haven't been seen for generations. Why have you come to us now?"

"We've come to help slow those that oppose us," Caldin began, then paused, turning to Sholin. "Does she have this effect on everyone? I couldn't stop myself from answering. That would be a tremendous political advantage in any realm."

Sholin nodded silently, mouthing "yes" as the dwarf continued.

"Vardon, how do you keep anything from her?" Caldin's grin widened. "Surely you've developed some talisman to ward off her effect."

"Unfortunately, it's not magic," Vardon chuckled. "Talismans are useless. You can build awareness of her effect and prepare your responses beforehand, but hide something from her?" He shook his head. "Impossible."

"I've brought a shipload of spark powder and an idea for..." Caldin stopped mid-sentence, eyes widening as he pointed toward the desk.

Everyone turned to look. A quill pen hovered in midair, suspended by nothing. Ellis placed a reassuring hand on Caldin's arm.

"Fear not. We're not haunted or bewitched. That's just my daughter letting us know she's here. Speak freely. The questers and the Mistress of Fire will hear our conversation."

Caldin's nervous laugh broke the tension. "Mistress of Fire?"

"She's been found," Ellis said. "Our quest has an astral someone not mentioned in any prophecy about these dark times." She gestured toward the floating pen. "Rika, this is Caldin Hardwfik, king of the Dwarves and protector of the seal. He brought us a gift and was explaining his plan."

Caldin stepped back, visibly startled. "I wasn't aware you had a daughter. Only sons were known to the realm. How did you conceal her existence?"

Ellis's knowing smile reached her eyes. "She's not truly my daughter, though I hope she will be when this is over. She was a Queen's Maid who encountered... difficulties... and had to leave the capital. During her journey, she met Blair and joined his quest." Her shoulders straightened with pride. "Perhaps it was fate that she discovered her talents just before meeting him."

Caldin bowed toward the floating pen. "Rika, a pleasure. Please convey my thanks to Prince Blair and to all risking their lives to save us." His expression turned serious.

"Now, Your Majesties, we'll need every cup and goblet you can spare, and several thousand men with shovels, hoes, and rakes. We're going to create a firestorm those creatures won't soon forget. It won't stop them, but it should give you an extra day to evacuate."

He began humming a battle tune under his breath, and Ellis, just as Sholin had predicted, threw her arms around the startled dwarf king.

The questers made camp as dusk settled over the rolling plains. Rika sank against her saddle with a weary sigh, her body aching from a day spent projecting her consciousness while on horseback. The constant vigilance checking for enemies, scouting paths ahead, returning to her body only to project again moments later had drained her completely.

She unfolded the worn pages Sholin had sent a diary from another Astral. Her fingers trembled slightly as she opened it. Finding others like herself had seemed impossible until now.

The first entry was simply dated: "Planting Season."

How can anybody not know what's happening to me? The handwriting was jagged, pressed deep into the parchment. For years they promised the Making would change my life. They never said change meant confusion and drifting through a fog of uncertainty.

Mother, that witch, she just smiles and says, "I don't know what it means, darling. Did you see the prince, though? How fortunate he got caught in that snowstorm. How regal he looked. We are so blessed."

Witch. Witch. WITCH.

What does it mean when I see myself walking while I float behind my body? How can they not see this? How am I supposed to marry when I don't even understand what I am? I'll end up like old Mabel, muttering to spirits no one else can see.

Rika's breath caught. The words could have been torn from her own thoughts. She turned the page to an entry marked "Harvest."

I killed Ben. I'm damned.

Dandy Sun Dancer carried me faithfully to two farms with seed bags. When I returned, I forgot to rub him down, remembering only after I was in bed.

I crept out to the stable in my night shift to give him extra grain. The stall gate opened behind me.

Heat flooded my face as I stood there, barely dressed. Ben stumbled in, caught himself, and looked at me with that crooked smile that wasn't a smile at all.

When he lunged, I jumped back. His hand caught my neck, tearing my shift. He grabbed my leg as I tried to escape, crawled on top of me, pinned me down. The stench of alcohol on his breath made me gag as I screamed.

When his hand grabbed my breast, something inside me... broke. I felt myself leave my body, floating above, watching as if through a window. His mouth was on me, and my floating self seized him by the hair.

"Die, you monster," I whispered, and he collapsed. Just... died.

I'm a murderer. I should kill myself before facing this shame. No one will marry me now. I should end this.

The diary slipped in Rika's hands. She felt Blair's presence before she saw him, his shadow falling over the page as he peered over her shoulder.

"Any help in there?" His voice was gentle, careful.

Rika closed the diary partway, her finger marking her place. "Apparently, I can command people to die simply by willing it." A nervous laugh escaped her lips. Not quite humor, not quite fear. "Isn't that special?"

Blair's eyes widened slightly. "I guess I should not make you angry, then." His light tone couldn't mask the flicker of concern. "I'll try to be exceptionally nice from now on."

She smiled weakly and returned to the diary, turning to an entry marked "Winter."

Matt Brady from Shingle Knoll smiled at me today. He has the kindest eyes.

I keep thinking I should end this life. He must know what I did. Everyone must.

They're sending me away, regardless. To Aster Hills and some mage named Erwin Summersault. They say she'll help, but it sounds like servitude to me.

They only believed my story about Ben because of my torn shift. No one will come near me now. They fear my touch. Perhaps death would be kinder.

The next entry showed steadier handwriting, dated a new "Planting Season."

Aurin Sweetwater is a good woman. Strict. Purposeful.

She opened her door, studied me from head to toe, then took my hand and looked directly into my eyes.

"It's his fault he's dead," she said. "You followed instinct and defended yourself. He attacked you. His fault, not yours."

A weight lifted from my heart. She hadn't even been told my name, yet she knew. A good woman.

I'm an Astral, she says. I can detach my consciousness and interact with the world. She has me practice constantly, says it builds control.

She'll call "OUT" from another room, and my floating self must find her.

She was furious when I pinched her, and she felt it. Apparently, I need only think of the sensation I want someone to feel, then make contact.

When she called out yesterday, I was washing dishes. I dropped a mug in surprise. Irritated, I pinched her backside when I found her. She jumped so high I couldn't help laughing.

She heard me laughing from the kitchen and turned scarlet. Now I'm only allowed to move objects in her sight. No touching.

I still smile, remembering how red her face got.

Today, I saw my parents! Aurin called me to her side, holding a making bell identical to the one in my bedroom.

"Picture your bell," she instructed. "Feel the room it sits in. Smell the air. Now go there."

Suddenly I stood in my bedroom, or my floating self did. I rushed to the kitchen where my parents sat at the table, looking worn and tired.

I felt thinner there, less substantial. I could barely affect anything.

Mother's flowers in the center of the table had wilted. I cupped them in my hands, breathed life into them.

Father sensed me. He whispered my name as the flowers slowly straightened in their vase.

Then I was back at Aurin's, breathless from the journey.

Rika lowered the diary, her mind racing. She had to try this. It was like finding the tree near Karen's family farm, focusing on a distant but familiar point.

She closed her eyes, picturing her childhood bedroom. The faded blue curtains her mother had sewn. The small wooden desk where she'd practiced her letters. The scent of lavender that always lingered in the corners.

With a gentle push, she stepped out of herself.

She was home. Everything exactly as she remembered. Her mother lay on the bed, face streaked with tears. Rika's heart clenched. She lay down beside her mother and wrapped her in an embrace, pouring every ounce of her energy into a single message: I'm safe with Prince Blair.

Her mother froze mid-sob. Her body tensed, then trembled. Rika held her, letting waves of emotion flow between them. Finally, she channeled the contentment she felt with Blair, the sense of purpose, the unexpected joy.

Her mother sat up suddenly, a smile of secret knowledge spreading across her face. She drew a deep breath, standing straighter than Rika had seen in years.

"Good for you," she whispered to the empty room. "Be safe. I love you."

Rika reached up, gently cradling her mother's head between her hands. The connection deepened, and her mother's worries crashed over her fear for her daughter, anger at the circumstances that took her away, pride in her resilience, and beneath it all, a love so vast and encompassing it made Rika's previous connections seem shallow by comparison. This differed from Merric's steady affection. This was primal, boundless.

Wondering if the difference lay in gender rather than relation, Rika sought her father. She found him at the kitchen table, quill scratching methodically across the ledger where he tracked the family's modest finances.

She approached cautiously. When she reached for his head, he looked up directly at her. He winked once, then returned to his figures as if such visitations were commonplace.

Rika drew back, startled. She rubbed her incorporeal hands together, gathering courage before reaching out again to touch his temples.

His mind startled her with its orderly simplicity. Do a task. Check if it was done correctly. Move to the next task. When she explored his feelings for her, she nearly broke the connection. He loved her still, but he loved the eight-year-old girl she had been, preserved perfectly in his memory, never changing, never growing.

The revelation stung. Rika pulled away and found herself back in the camp, tears streaming down her face. Blair knelt beside her, one hand hovering near her face. "You're back," he whispered, relief evident in the lines around his eyes. "What did you see?"

She leaned into his touch briefly, then straightened her spine. "Mother knows I'm alive now." Her voice cracked. "Father... mourns a ghost."

She ran a hand through her hair, frustration kindling. "Sholin gave me this…" she gestured at the journal, "… but Aurin teaches me parlor tricks. Pinching and whispering. What is she afraid I'll discover?"

Her eyes met Blair's, no longer afraid but determined. "The unknown Astral killed a man who tried to harm her. She visited her family across vast distances." Rika's voice hardened. "I need the full truth of what I am. Not just what's convenient for others."

The diary lay open between them, its warnings clear in the firelight.

CHAPTER 17

THE BROKEN COVENANT

The path dissolved beneath their horses' hooves as they followed a creek winding between hills draped in evergreens. Amber-flowered grasses with needle-sharp thorns grew thigh-high along the slopes, catching at clothing like grasping hands. Shandar rode slightly apart, studying the hills' unnatural symmetry. Not hills, mounds. Ancient and deliberate.

Nine travelers moved through the landscape, sometimes single file, sometimes paired. Voices rose and fell in quiet conversation. Shandar wondered how they would recognize their destination when Reid suddenly veered left onto a dirt path strewn with rocks. No vegetation grew there, as if the earth itself had been scorched clean.

Ahead, the evergreens pressed so close they formed a tunnel of interlaced limbs. Blair raised his hand. The company halted. Reid continued several paces before noticing and turned back, confusion etched on his face. Blair silenced him with an upraised palm.

"Rika, would you check?" Blair's gaze lifted to the tunnel's ceiling where branches twisted into patterns too precise to be natural.

Rika exhaled sharply. Shandar glanced over, expecting irritation, but found Rika watching her with a knowing smile. Only then did Shandar realize she'd been lost in thought, still processing their earlier merge.

Without a word, Rika slipped the Star from beneath her tunic and placed it around her neck. Her eyes closed, her back straightened, and her body went still while her spirit ventured forth.

"Power surrounds this place," she reported, voice distant. "It shimmers but does nothing. It waits." A pause. "I'm entering the tunnel now."

Silence fell. Minutes stretched. The horses shifted uneasily beneath them. When Rika's eyes finally opened, they shone with an inner light that wasn't entirely human.

"It comes from the mound," she whispered, voice trembling with wonder. "Massive power, countless veins flowing outward. All dormant." She hesitated. "Waiting for something." Her gaze locked on Blair. "There are no people within a quarter day's ride. We should proceed."

The formal report delivered, she turned to Shandar, eyes suddenly bright. "You must see it from the spirit plane," she whispered, leaning closer. "It's beautiful beyond words. May I show you?"

The eagerness in Rika's voice caught Shandar off guard. Their earlier merge had been intense, intimate in ways that left her feeling exposed. Yet the warmth in Rika's smile made refusal impossible.

"Show me," Shandar said, reaching for Rika's arm.

The merge began with that familiar double awareness, two souls occupying one space. Then boundaries dissolved. Rika's essence flowed into her, courage facing danger, goodness despite fear, vulnerability beneath confidence. Here was the life Shandar had longed for: family, purpose, belonging. Tears slipped down her cheeks as she surrendered to the connection.

Rika guided them to the crossroads facing the mound. From the spirit plane, its true nature revealed itself, a massive jewel cut with five precise faces, inverted and partially concealed by vegetation. Its flat top angled skyward, as if waiting for a particular star.

From its summit poured a waterfall of light. Luminous veins in shifting colors cascaded down each face, merging and separating in patterns too complex to follow. All except one. A single vein remained constant, its color a perfect match to the fire burning within Shandar's chest. Without conscious thought, she moved toward it, drawing Rika along. When her spirit-self touched the vein, power surged through her, ancient, familiar, hungry.

It's mine, she thought. It has always been mine.

We must go back, Rika's voice echoed in her mind.

But the power, can't you feel it?

That's why we must go. A shudder passed through Rika's essence.

Something within the mound stirred. A presence, vast and ancient, turned its attention toward them. The constant vein pulsed once, reaching for Shandar like a finger of flame.

Awareness crashed back like a physical blow. Shandar swayed in her saddle, disoriented. A hollow emptiness spread through her chest where Rika's presence had been. Can I stop her from leaving if I try? The thought came unbidden, disturbing in its possessiveness. Something of Shandar had gone with Rika in the separation, leaving a void that ached to be filled.

"That was a gift," said Finrod, suddenly beside her. His head tilted as he studied her face, ancient eyes seeing more than Shandar wished to reveal. "To see magic in its flows on the spirit plane." He placed a steadying hand on her arm. "You can train yourself to see them in the physical world now. Remember what you've seen. The memory will guide your sight."

His mouth turned down, forming that peculiar pout that made him look centuries younger. "You are a marvel, Shandar Corpus. With your sister at your side, you may be unstoppable."

As Finrod rode toward the tunnel, Shandar smiled despite the lingering emptiness. Rika waited patiently ahead, but something had changed between them, a connection forged, yes, but also a boundary crossed. Shandar could still feel the pull of that steady vein of power, calling to her like a forgotten name.

The tunnel wasn't solid, gaps showed where trees had died or been struck by lightning, yet the weight of it pressed down as they rode through in somber silence. Branches seemed to reach lower with each passing moment. No one spoke, but tension hung in the air like the moment before lightning strikes.

The tunnel ended several paces from the crossroads. The company halted, all eyes drawn to the mound.

Shandar turned to share the moment with Rika, only to find her staring intently at Blair's rigid back. She tugged Rika's reins.

"Copper for your thoughts?" Shandar asked.

"It's Blair," Rika whispered, voice tight. "He's angry, and it's affecting all of us." Her eyes narrowed. "Something must be done."

"You have some way to help him?" Shandar studied Rika's face. "What makes you so certain he's angry?"

Rika's mouth opened, then closed without sound. Something flickered behind her eyes, knowledge she wasn't ready to share. "I don't know how to handle this," she admitted finally.

Shandar considered the group dynamics, the patterns of deference. "Merric," she said simply.

Rika straightened, eyes widening. "Of course. That's the relationship I overlooked. Authoritarian, but tempered with affection and respect." A smile spread across her face. "You're brilliant. I'll speak with him at camp."

Before Shandar could respond, Rika had already moved her horse toward Merric. The loss of her presence left Shandar oddly bereft. She guided her mount to Blair's side, earning a smile that didn't reach his eyes.

"Rika," Blair called, "did you see any suitable campsites during your spirit walk?"

"I'm sorry," Rika replied, unable to meet his gaze. "I was completely absorbed by the mound's magic. There is a larger creek at the northeast corner."

"That would be the Feder," Reid confirmed. "There's a good campsite there."

Blair nodded. "Merric, take Bal and Ras right along the mound. Scout ahead but stay within sight. We'll meet at the campsite."

Merric acknowledged with a wave and set off. Rika immediately followed, calling, "I'll go with Merric."

"And I'll join Rika," Kumar added, spurring his horse after them.

Finrod glanced at Blair, who merely shrugged and turned left. Shandar moved to ride at his side, rewarded with another smile, warmer this time. The pull of the mound's power faded as they distanced themselves from it, but Shandar could still feel it pulsing at the edge of her awareness.

The campsite showed signs of centuries of use, a semi-circle of evergreens sheltering a clearing with a well-established fire pit. The Feder's clear waters flowed just forty paces beyond the trees.

Shandar helped gather firewood, and soon they were all seated around the crackling flames, exchanging stories as they waited for the others.

When the scouting party finally arrived, Rika's mood was clearly plain. She rode several lengths ahead, her face dark as a gathering storm. A man did that, Shandar thought instinctively, rising to meet her at the picket line.

She took the reins from the men and began unsaddling their mounts while Rika attacked her own horse's coat with short, angry strokes of the brush. Shandar watched for a moment before intervening.

"It's not Spartan's fault you're upset," she said quietly. "Be gentle with him."

Rika froze mid-stroke, shoulders rigid. Then she wrapped her arms around the horse's neck, murmuring an apology. Spartan kicked twice with his front hoof, accepting her contrition.

She resumed grooming with gentler hands. Shandar unsaddled the remaining horse and began brushing him down, both women working longer than necessary, the animals forming a barrier between them. Finally, Shandar broke the silence.

"I take it Merric wasn't helpful?"

"'Anger is better than despair,'" Rika quoted bitterly. "Can you believe that's what he said? I nearly slapped him for being so..." She struggled for words. "...so male." Her hands clenched into fists. "He wants to let Blair handle it alone. As if he doesn't even care."

Her boot kicked at the earth, sending pebbles scattering.

Shandar considered her response carefully, feeling the emptiness inside her where Rika's presence had been.

Part of her wanted to agree, to share Rika's indignation and bind them closer. Instead, she said, "Merric cares deeply for Blair. You're upset with his approach, not his intentions."

She stroked the horse's flank methodically, feeling the animal's warmth against her palm. "Men often carry their burdens differently. Perhaps his advice has merit. You can only influence what's within your control."

She met Rika's eyes across the horses' backs. "Be kind to Blair. Watch how he processes this. Support him. Believe in him."

Those last three words carried more weight than the rest. Rika studied Shandar, her expression softening as she recalled their shared consciousness.

"You're right," Rika admitted. "I do believe in him. I just wish..." She sighed. "I wish he would handle his emotions the way I think he should. Is that terribly selfish?"

"Perhaps a little," Shandar said with a small smile. "But your concern comes from caring."

Rika moved around the horses and embraced Shandar tightly. "Thank you, sister," she whispered against Shandar's ear. "I love you."

The words settled into Shandar's heart like a balm against the hollow ache that had lingered since their separation. But as they walked back toward the fire, Shandar glanced over her shoulder toward the mound, just visible in the gathering darkness. The constant vein of power was still there, she knew, waiting. Calling to her. And someday soon, she would answer.

Two days of searching had hollowed Rika to her core. The Star of Serenity hung from her neck like an executioner's stone, siphoning her life with each labored heartbeat.

"Almost there," she whispered, voice barely a rasp as she stumbled over roots. Her green eyes had dulled to tarnished copper. Sweat plastered hair to her ashen face despite the cool night. The Star's silver glow had faded to match her dwindling strength.

When her legs betrayed her, Rika collapsed onto the moss. The cool earth against her palms offered small comfort. She closed her eyes, reaching for even a flicker of Astral power. Pain lanced through her skull.

"Lashnar," she prayed through cracked lips, fingers clutching the Star. "Guide me."

Though her body failed, something within refused surrender. Monde's fate rested partly on her shoulders. In the stillness, she sensed the faintest energy, a tiny ember refusing to die. Not much, but enough.

Kumar hadn't left Rika's side, his elvish features tight with concern as he tended the fire. The failed search had cast a pall over camp.

"We grid-walk the mound at dawn," Arbor suggested, voice low. "Section by section."

Blair moved around the fire, filling cups with watered wine. As he bent to serve Rasslow, a golden medallion slipped from his shirt, catching firelight.

Finrod's eyes widened. "Nuuta botuu, haaku!" He slammed his palm against his forehead. "The medallion, we never used it!"

Everyone froze.

"I've been distracted," Finrod continued, glancing toward Shandar. "Those two girls merged could move horses and riders across all of Monde in a heartbeat. The medallion alone might suffice." His hand clenched. "Give it to me. Arbor, Kumar, follow."

Kumar hesitated, looking at Rika's sleeping form.

"She's safe," Blair said. "Go."

Blair passed the medallion to Finrod, who held it by its chain and spun it with his fingers. "Faroth Coron Torrech Fae Hir-Si Mi Si."

The medallion jerked, then shot toward the mound like an arrow. Kumar and Arbor sprinted after it, disappearing into the twilight.

Finrod turned to Shandar. "What you just witnessed was an incantation. It limits the scope, requires less power, and has minimal effect on the surrounding environment."

"What did you say?" Shandar asked, brow furrowed.

"Hunt mound, lair spirit, find this," Finrod translated with a small smile. "I don't use full sentences. The medallion responds to both words and thoughts."

Kumar burst through the trees. "We found it! A dead oak, the medallion fit perfectly into a slot. The glamor's gone. There's a door."

Everyone rose except Kumar, who moved to Rika's side with his kettle. "I'll stay until her strength returns. Bring Dagmar here when the deal is done."

Reid shifted to the farthest side of the fire, eyeing Rika. "I'll keep watch," he muttered, though everyone knew he simply couldn't stomach sickness.

Kumar brewed tea from herbs in his pouch, roused Rika enough for a few sips. She drifted back to sleep. He settled beside her, watching her chest rise and fall, wondering what price they would pay for Dagmar's help.

Blair lingered at the edge of camp, watching Kumar tend to Rika before hurrying after the others. They stood before an alcove cut with impossible precision into the mound, a straight slice creating an overhang two paces deep.

Beneath hung a wooden door with an iron handle. Beside it sat a birch pot containing a cypress topiary trimmed into a perfect spiral, impossibly green and vital. The contrast against the dead oak and wild forest was jarring, like finding a palace parlor in wilderness.

Blair approached the door.

"Stop," Finrod hissed, chewing his cheek. "It's his home. Knock first."

Blair squared his shoulders and rapped his knuckles against the wood. Silence stretched until the door swung inward.

Light spilled from above, illuminating the occupant. Tall and lithe, with muscles like corded tendons beneath fern-colored fur. An inverted triangular face with a small round chin rising to prominent cheekbones. Mismatched eyes caught the light—one emerald, one pale blue, beneath a patch of bare skull. A ruddy mane cascaded down his back.

"Ya do remember you're on a qu'est, no?" The creature's lip curled, revealing needle-sharp teeth. "Ya have the medallion but don't use it for two days? I thought I'd have to open the damn thing myself."

He wore what could only be described as a bathrobe tied loosely at his narrow waist. His black, cat-like whiskers twitched with irritation.

"Where's the girl with the Star?" he demanded. "Who taught her magic? She nearly died wearing herself down like that."

Blair's posture stiffened as realization hit him. Two days of searching, two days of Rika fading to nothing, when they had the means to find Dagmar all along.

"She's resting in camp," he managed. "The Star drains her."

"Who taught her? A novice?"

"Herself," Blair answered, unable to suppress a grim smile at his companions' surprise.

Dagmar disappeared inside without another word. Grunts and clatters echoed from within.

Minutes later, he emerged wearing midnight-black armor that matched Shandar's. A sword with a crescent moon handle hung over his shoulder. He brushed past Blair toward camp.

Shandar intercepted him, blocking his path. Dagmar stopped, mismatched eyes studying her. Then he stepped forward, took her hand, and knelt.

"Mistress," he said formally, "you wear your mantle better than I hoped. I am your servant." He kissed her hand, rose, and continued toward camp.

They followed in silence. As they approached the fire, Kumar moved protectively in front of Rika. Dagmar slowed, stopping where he could clearly see her.

Kumar's smile held no warmth.

Then Dagmar changed.

His body flowed like water in a vessel. Waist narrowed, shoulders rounded, small breasts formed beneath the now-ill-fitting sword belt. A five-foot tail grew from his spine, tipped with crimson hair. His neck thinned, features softened, ruddy mane transforming to royal blue. She stretched upward, revealing webbing that extended from wrists to pelvis.

Kumar's jaw slackened. Even Blair stared.

The fairy bowed. "An elf guarding a human mage. Does she know how special that is?" Her voice chimed like crystal. "I am Salem. May I heal her?"

Kumar nodded, speechless.

Salem placed her hand on Rika's forehead. Cornflower blue light emanated from her palm, spreading in a gentle halo before flowing down Rika's body like liquid starlight.

Rika's eyes fluttered open. "Whoa," she gasped, "a gentle shake would have sufficed." She pushed up on her elbows, glanced at Kumar reproachfully, then froze at the sight of Salem.

"Dagmar?" she whispered.

Salem's laugh rippled through the air. "No, child. I am Salem, Dagmar's other half. I heal; he will teach you to use the Star without being drained." She tilted her head. "How do you feel?"

Rika began to answer, then gasped. "Quite well. Your doing?" She stretched, then in one fluid motion rose, spun in a circle, and planted her feet wide apart. Color had returned to her cheeks, her eyes bright again.

She hugged herself, eyes closed in appreciation, then tilted sideways and landed on the ground with a thump.

"Food before acrobatics," Kumar said, appearing with broth. "Your body needs time."

Rika accepted the pot. After the first sip, she squeezed Kumar's hand in thanks.

"You are a delightful enigma," Salem said, leaning forward. "Who are you?"

"Rika Gresso. Small-town girl, Queen's Maid, law breaker, outlaw, Astral, and companion to my friends." She glanced around. "Where is Dagmar? Can I meet him?"

Salem doubled over with laughter. As she recovered, Blair and Shandar settled beside Rika. Salem sat cross-legged before them.

"I am Salem," she said to Shandar and Blair. "As for meeting Dagmar, you already have. We are hermaphrodite, shifting between male and female forms. I am Salem, but I am also part of the mind you know as Dagmar. Speaking to me is speaking to him." She turned her palms upward. "Shall we discuss our deal?"

Rika glanced at Shandar, then Blair. Both nodded.

"What was the price of your last deal?" Blair asked, suddenly grave.

"Defining parameters to gauge the cost... a true Prince." Salem's iridescent eyes bored into Blair. "Our home has served us well these seven hundred seasons." She glanced around. "I would like all to hear this. Their lives will be affected too."

"Around the fire, then," Blair said, offering Shandar his hand. She took it with visible reluctance.

The group formed a circle around the embers. Rasslow and Baltan tried to remain by the horses until Blair beckoned them firmly.

"All of us. This concerns everyone."

When they were assembled, only fire crackle and night birds broke the silence. Blair nodded to Salem.

"We stand at a crossroads," she began, her voice dropping to command attention. "Darkness, betrayal, and death lie ahead. An evil unseen for thousands of seasons has awakened. Triangul now rises before dawn. Time works against us."

Her eyes reflected firelight. "You need Dagmar, Golden Heart and Friend to All, to reach your destination. Your prophecy demands it."

She pushed up her sleeves deliberately. "Victory is what our deal plans for. Dagmar, however, does not plan on surviving."

A collective breath caught in throats around the fire.

"He is a warrior," Salem continued, "but no wars have been fought for generations. He stands in the evening of his dream and wishes only for peace."

She stared at her empty hands, then inhaled deeply, shoulders swaying as though to music only she heard.

"I want to live as a single being. To explore these lands as I never have before." Her voice softened. "I am an elemental. My mere presence affects what surrounds me."

She weighed each word. "If I turned evil, I would become terrible. I don't believe I'm evil, but I cannot guarantee that for all time." Her eyes met each of theirs. "It's a risk, just as allowing an enemy to live is a risk. Humans do this constantly. The risk is minor. The requirement... is heavy."

"Heavy is the burden placed on oneself," Finrod murmured, smile brittle.

Salem nodded. "Separating from Dagmar requires enormous power and many components." She paused, letting silence build. "Our deal hinges on one critical ingredient: a human egg."

Blair's head jerked back. "A human... egg?" The words came as a whisper.

"To grow a new body for me," Salem said matter-of-factly.

The fire popped loudly. Merric coughed. Baltan and Rasslow exchanged bewildered glances.

Rika's face had gone pale. "Does the egg's age matter? Could it be from a woman near the end of her cycles?"

"Age is of no consequence."

"Physical presence is necessary?"

"Yes. She must be present for the spell."

"And your relationship with the woman afterward?"

"Blood kin. Cousins, in your terminology."

Rika turned away. "We need time. We will come to your home with our answer."

Salem rose in one fluid motion. "Bring the woman or don't come." Her voice hardened. "Once you leave the forest barrier, you'll be sensed again. The forces controlled by this evil will find you shortly after." Her eyes softened. "I want to live. Remember that."

She floated away, gradually fading into darkness.

Silence stretched, heavy with unspoken thoughts. They gathered closer, standing in a tight circle. Blair's shoulders hunched under leadership's weight.

"Can we ask our women to give up their firstborn for this?" he asked, gaze moving between Rika and Shandar, pain etched around his eyes.

Shandar turned away, back to the mound. Her lips pressed into a line as she shook her head, one hand covering her mouth.

"No," she whispered. "Neither of us should be forced into this."

Finrod's smile wavered. "I agree. Though Golden Heart is named in my version of the prophecy as well. His help would be... valuable."

Blair's gaze skipped around the circle, body restless.

"Does it have to be them?" Merric asked. "Can't we find someone else?" He turned to Rika. "You had something in mind with those questions."

But Rika stood motionless, eyes closed, consciousness elsewhere despite not wearing the Star.

The others settled back down. Shandar slumped onto a stump, her eyes suddenly glazing over. Blair watched with concern, guessing that Rika had somehow reached out to her.

Minutes passed. Rika inhaled sharply and staggered backward.

None of them noticed the figure that had materialized beside Shandar.

"Whoa, that was strange," said a melodious voice.

Blair spun around, heart stopping. "Mom?"

Queen Ellis Whyte-Willow stood among them, unescorted and radiant even in dim firelight. Blair moved as in a dream, crossing to her in three strides before enfolding her in his arms. He lifted her off the ground, face buried in her shoulder.

"I didn't know how much I needed to see you," he whispered, voice breaking. Setting her down, he dropped to his knees, forehead pressed against her middle.

Merric remained seated, chuckling softly, shaking his head with affection.

The Queen guided Blair to his feet and turned toward Shandar. With practiced grace, she curtsied.

"Mistress, it is an honor to serve you. I am Ellis Whyte-Willow, Queen."

Shandar's mouth snapped shut. She bowed awkwardly. "We serve each other, Your Majesty."

The Queen's smile was like sunrise after a long night. Shandar straightened, growing taller under that approving gaze. Beside them, Rika's eyes filled with tears as the Queen embraced her.

"It's alright, daughter," Ellis whispered, just loud enough for those nearest to hear.

Composing herself, Ellis turned to her son. "Introductions?"

Blair offered his arm, guiding her toward the elves. "Prince Finrod of the Mountain Elves, may I present Queen Ellis Whyte-Willow, my mother." He gestured to the others. "His companions, Kumar and Arbor."

Finrod bowed. "Your beauty rivals the greatest sunset. Tales did not do justice to reality."

They exchanged formal bows, acknowledgment between equals. Kumar and Arbor knelt in respect.

Ellis embraced Merric with genuine warmth.

"I told you that girl would bring me here," Merric laughed.

"Impossible imp," the Queen retorted, joining his laughter.

Blair introduced the guardsmen. They saluted, fists crossing their chests.

Rasslow stepped forward. "Your Majesty, we mean no disrespect, but the Mistress is who we follow now. Would you allow us this freedom?"

He knelt, lowering his head. Baltan followed. A hush fell over the camp.

Ellis touched each man lightly on the head before bidding them rise.

"My duty is to protect this land and its people," she said. "Allowing you to serve the Mistress of Fire fulfills that duty." Her eyes twinkled. "Now you'll have no objections when I take Merric with me." She glanced around. "Is there wine? And..." her gaze settled on Rika, "...why am I here?"

The men collectively retreated from her question. Rika stepped forward with wine.

"Your Majesty, would you walk with us? Shandar and I will explain by the river. The sound of rushing water provides privacy."

Ellis accepted the cup, allowing herself to be guided toward the river. Once seated on smooth stones at the water's edge, the three women regarded one another, nervousness evident in averted gazes.

Rika took a deep breath. "We were informed by Aurin Sweetwater that the Golden Heart mentioned in the prophecy is Dagmar, a fairy warrior. To secure his help, we must strike a bargain."

She explained about the fairies' nature, their desire to separate, and Salem's powers.

"Dagmar intends to die helping us. Salem healed me and says Dagmar can teach me to use the Star without being drained."

"The Star?" Ellis inquired, eyebrow raised.

"Another gift from Aurin," Rika admitted. "It allows me to see through magic and communicate when my spirit leaves my body. Using it without cost would be invaluable before we confront this evil."

Ellis raised her hand, silencing further explanation. She turned toward the river, its dark waters gleaming with starlight. For several moments, she simply listened to night sounds, breathing measured as she gathered her thoughts.

Ellis stared at Rika, comprehension dawning slowly. "Men acting shy... the only woman here." Her voice strengthened. "They want a baby? You want me to find them a baby?"

Rika shook her head, unable to meet the Queen's eyes. "No. Are you..." She swallowed. "Are you still having cycles, Your Majesty?"

Ellis's hand flew to her throat. She turned away, shoulders rigid. "You want me to have a baby?" Her voice began thin and brittle. "Have you lost your mind?"

"Mother," Rika's voice softened, "one of us three must give up an egg. The magic requires it. They'll use it to grow Salem into her separate self."

"So, it's to be me?" Ellis's laugh was hollow. She slumped on the riverbank, suddenly older. "Are you that shrewd, child? Do you already see the advantage of binding fairy magic to the royal line?"

"No." Rika's eyes glistened. "I couldn't bear to give up my firstborn. And I couldn't ask Shandar to do what I wasn't willing to do myself." She reached toward Ellis but stopped short. "I knew you were the answer."

Ellis studied both young women. The mask of queenship slipped, revealing something raw beneath. She pressed her palm against her abdomen, still strong despite the years and children it had carried. Her brow furrowed. She bit her lip, eyes darting toward the dark river as if seeking escape.

Then something shifted. Her jaw firmed. She straightened her spine, and when she met their gaze again, resolve had hardened in her eyes.

"Quite the trap you've laid." Ellis's voice was dry. "I suppose consulting Vardon is out of the question?" She looked between them. "We're a quarter-moon from the castle being attacked. We have preparations. The capital will be abandoned for Tiereny."

Shandar remained still, save for her searching eyes. Rika's mouth fell open.

"It doesn't have to be you," Rika said, voice lower than before, "but it can't be us." The fight had drained from her face, leaving only exhaustion and pleading eyes.

"Give Blair what he needs, and you save all the children." Shandar tipped her head back, blinking at stars. "Both the elves and Blair believe we need Dagmar." She looked directly at Ellis, deference at odds with intensity. "Your Majesty, please."

As Shandar closed her eyes in silent prayer, Ellis's features sagged. The weight of a realm pressed on her shoulders, as it always had.

"Very well," she said. "Let's do this."

Blair kept his distance as the three women approached Dagmar's dwelling. Each crunch of gravel beneath his boots echoed his heartbeat. He'd already lost the argument about being here, both with Shandar, who insisted he shouldn't witness this, and with his mother, who'd dismissed his concerns with brutal simplicity: his presence would change nothing.

What would be, would be.

Yet he couldn't leave her to face this alone. Too many grimoires in his father's library detailed magical ceremonies gone horrifically wrong.

Rika glanced back, golden hair slicing across her shoulder. The question in her eyes needed no voice: Still with us? Shandar's jaw worked silently, fingers drumming a nervous rhythm against her staff. Between them walked Queen Ellis, her cloak whispering around her ankles as she fixed her gaze on the open doorway ahead.

The entrance was cut directly into the hillside, framed by cypress wood with runes pulsing blue at its threshold. Blair allowed himself a small smile at this ordinary detail, a doorframe, amidst such extraordinary circumstances.

Inside, Ellis raised one hand. Light bloomed instantly from iron sconces, revealing a chamber that defied the mound's exterior dimensions. Blair swallowed hard. Honeyed sandstone columns soared upward, their surfaces writhing with carved vines. The wedge-shaped space funneled attention to three stone pedestals beneath a broad arch, with curved stairs ascending on either side.

Salem lounged against the central altar, one boot propped against its base. At their entrance, she straightened, hope flickering across her sharp features before she masked it behind formality. The women climbed toward her. When Blair moved to follow, Salem raised a single hand. He stopped.

"You've decided?" Salem's voice carried clearly in the vaulted chamber, her eyes finding Ellis. "You'll grant our petition?"

Ellis mounted the lowest step, her cloak pooling around her. Salem bowed, then spoke with deliberate formality.

"My Lady, you honor our home." She turned to Rika. "And the farm girl who's earned a queen's ear." She guided Ellis toward the right pedestal with a sweeping gesture. "Do you comprehend what stands before you? Alone, this child wields remarkable power. Combined with the Mistress…" Her voice softened. "How did you come to know her?"

"She slapped my son." Ellis's diplomatic mask slipped into something genuine. "I decided not to kill her."

Salem's laugh burst forth, unexpected and musical. She positioned Ellis beside the right pedestal, then addressed her with gentler tones.

"Lie here. I'll take the left, with the Itatiella pod between us." She explained the process with the care of a physician. "A dream-haze will take you. You'll remain conscious but unable to move. When you wake, I'll occupy the center, Dagmar the left." Her voice caught slightly. "You'll feel lightheaded, then… nothing." She paused. "Thank you."

Rika's fingers worked at her cuticles. Shandar's hand hovered near her staff. Ellis smoothed her skirts and reclined on the cold stone as if it were merely an uncomfortable bed at a diplomatic function.

Salem approached the glowing pod. From a leather pouch, she extracted pale powder and sprinkled it over the surface. Without ceremony, she lay down on her own slab.

"Zanna Xantho," she whispered.

A sharp chirp split the silence. Smoke coiled from the pod, dividing and enveloping both women. Their bodies tensed once, then went slack. The smoke thickened, transforming to a silvery gel that draped them like burial shrouds.

A red pinpoint appeared over Ellis's heart.

Blair's throat closed. The crimson essence, his mother's fertility, her sacrifice, drifted across the gap between pedestals and sank into the pod's core.

Rika seized Shandar's hand. Their eyes unfocused simultaneously, seeing beyond the physical. Blair could only watch as they gasped at whatever magical currents were visible to them alone.

The pod lifted from its pedestal. Its shell liquefied, dripping pearlescent fluid that devoured the stone beneath. Blair climbed one step higher, straining to see his mother. Above them all, a prismatic dome cascaded with rainbow light.

He watched, transfixed, as the pod and Salem blurred together into living light. Magic poured between them, a torrent from Salem to the pod, a thin trickle from Ellis.

On the left pedestal, a form solidified, Dagmar, unconscious but intact. Bands of amber energy arced from him to the central mass.

The sphere flared vermillion, so bright Blair had to shield his eyes. When he looked again, the light had softened to cream, then winked out entirely.

Three figures remained: Dagmar, Ellis, and between them on the floor, a new woman with cream-pale skin threaded with vermillion currents. Her hair, once Salem's fiery red, now shone golden as summer wheat.

Blair rushed down the stairs and dropped to his knees beside his mother. Her pulse beat steady beneath his fingertips. She opened her eyes and squeezed his hand.

"I'm fine," she whispered. "Thank you for staying."

On the floor, the new Salem stirred. She curled into herself, hugging her knees to her chest, then looked up at Dagmar with sage-green eyes.

"I miss your voice in my mind," she said. "I thought I would feel... complete. Do you miss me?"

"Lass," Dagmar's voice roughened with emotion, "not hearing your nagging is the only reason I agreed to this."

He pulled her to her feet and into an embrace that spoke of centuries shared. When the moment stretched too long, Blair cleared his throat. They broke apart, both flushing. Dagmar clasped his hands behind his back, military-straight.

"We should return," he said gruffly. "There's much to prepare before dawn."

Outside, the company froze mid-activity as Ellis emerged. She leaned briefly on Blair's arm before straightening, brushing an errant curl from her face, and giving the camp a regal nod. Activity resumed with the quiet efficiency of those accustomed to royal presence.

Ellis slipped her arm through Blair's as they approached the fire. "It was terrifying at first," she murmured, eyes closing against the memory. "I couldn't move... couldn't breathe. Then came peace. Perfect peace." Her smile carried a shadow. "And then you were there."

She didn't speak of what she'd sacrificed. She never would. Queens bear their burdens silently.

Across the fire, Shandar, Rika, and the newly-formed Salem huddled together, heads bent in whispered consultation.

Dagmar drained a cup of wine Merric had handed him. "We march at first light," he announced, voice carrying across the camp. "Two days to the Squat Hills, then over the waste to Dragon Rest." Without another word, he strode away, back rigid. Salem rose, squeezed both girls' hands, and followed.

Shandar leaned toward Rika. "Let's check if the Queen's chambers are empty."

Rika closed her eyes, her consciousness stretching across miles. "Clear," she confirmed, opening her eyes.

Merric embraced Rika, pressing a kiss to her forehead. "Be smart," he murmured. "Let others help you."

Shandar's fingers traced a complex pattern in the air. Golden light shimmered, and Ellis and Merric simply vanished.

Blair exhaled shakily. "They're safe. My mothers by the fire, eyes closed." He hugged Rika with fierce gratitude.

Dagmar spun toward them, wine sloshing from his cup. "Flippin' insane!" he sputtered. "Whisking people about like that!" His face darkened. "How?"

Shandar nodded toward Rika, who stretched out on the ground like a starfish.

"Magic is wish fulfillment," Rika said, her voice dreamy as her fingers wove patterns in the air. "I believe, therefore it is."

"You could destroy everything!" Dagmar's breathing grew labored, his face flushing dark. He looked desperately toward Salem. "Are you hearing this madness?"

Salem stepped between them, her posture fluid as water. "New generations bring new understanding," she said, her voice melodic but firm. "It's why she's here. We must grow with her or be left behind."

Her hand brushed Dagmar's arm. "Rest now. The journey begins at dawn."

Dagmar's shoulders slumped as he turned away, disappearing into shadow. Around the fire, the company settled onto their blankets. Rika and Shandar pressed close, sharing secret smiles in the firelight.

"He thinks he's leading this quest," Shandar murmured.

Rika's eyes caught the ember-light. "How do we tell a centuries-old fairy warrior that he isn't in charge?"

Shandar's grin turned dangerous in the dying light. "Carefully."

CHAPTER 18

THE FALL OF CRENWELGE

A rooster's cry split the gray dawn, cut short by a panicked squawk as rough hands stuffed it into a cage. King Vardon didn't turn. From atop the East tower, he watched the sun's first rays illuminate his nightmare: dust clouds rolling across the plains, swallowing the horizon.

A hundred thousand mouths to feed on the move. His fingers tightened on the stone parapet until his knuckles whitened. Not just refugees. Every soul within these walls.

Merric had been right to send Ellis across the river. If today went as badly as he feared, and it would, at least she might live. The thought of a world without her made his chest constrict.

If she died before me, I wouldn't last a season. He closed his eyes briefly. I'd follow her into darkness and let this world burn.

A quiver toppled behind him, arrows clattering across stone. Vardon turned to face two rows of archers lining the wall, nearly a thousand, most with trembling hands. Only the elite Sites stood steady. Between them, braziers waited, flames hungry.

"They're here," whispered a page. The boy's voice cracked like autumn ice.

Vardon's jaw tightened. "So they are."

Through morning haze, shapes emerged six hundred paces out. Warrior-mages glided forward with inhuman grace, arranging themselves across the King's Road with practiced precision. Behind them came two wagons, each pulled by straining oxen.

Vardon's mouth went dry as he made out crude X-shaped frames atop the wagons. From each hung a figure, arms stretched beyond human limits.

Then came the beast: massive and gray, flanks like stone, legs like pillars. Its trunk lifted, releasing a trumpet so deep the tower stones vibrated beneath Vardon's feet.

On its back sat a rider, muscular, horned, every inch the monster from children's nightmares. Nudzh. The creature circled the wagons once, then halted directly between them, framed by the bloody sunrise.

Nudzh gestured. The mages began to weave spells, and the suspended figures on the wagons expanded in Vardon's vision until he could see every detail. The collective intake of breath along the wall was like wind through dead leaves.

Prince Saad on the left. Commander Andreas on the right.

Their faces were maps of torture, bruises layered upon bruises, dried blood catching morning light. Their heads hung at unnatural angles. Royal garments hung in charred tatters.

"Gods above," someone whispered.

Nudzh raised one clawed hand. His voice crashed across the plain: "Surrender the King and Queen, and this city will be spared."

Behind him, the true army appeared, a black tide flowing from the east, north, and south. Warriors moved in eerie silence save for the whisper of leather and metal. They encircled the walls like a noose.

Vardon stumbled back against the tower wall. Two hundred thousand, at least. Still coming.

Now he saw the creatures clearly, seven feet tall with shoulders broader than any human's, tapering to narrow waists. Coarse black hair covered their arms and faces. Their halberds glowed with sickly green fire.

A murmur of despair rippled through the garrison. Vardon recognized the sound of men about to break.

"You!" He pointed to the nearest archer, whose face went ash-white. "Are you a Site?"

The man straightened. "No, Your Majesty. Fair shot but not designated."

"Your orders have changed." Vardon gripped the man's shoulder. "Run to the river. Tell them time has ended. Abandon everything and flee inland until your lungs burn. We'll hold this wall as long as we draw breath." His fingers dug into the archer's shoulder. "Make Merric hear every word. Go!"

The archer dropped his bow and fled.

"I am Nudzh," the monster called, voice echoing off the walls, "anointed doom to House Willow. Your gates remain closed. You have squandered your chance."

He flicked his hand. The mages turned back to the wagons and began a new chant.

On the right frame, Andreas convulsed. His head snapped up, eyes wide with animal terror. A scream tore from his throat as the flesh at his shoulders began to melt, running down his chest in rivulets. Wherever the fluid touched, more flesh dissolved. His screams built as skin vanished, revealing glistening ribs, snapping tendons. His arms tore free, hanging like trophies while what remained of him collapsed.

For one heartbeat, the world fell silent.

"Open the gates," Nudzh demanded, "or is your remaining son's life not worth yours?"

Every defender looked to Vardon. The king's legs failed him; he dropped to one knee.

Forgive me, Andreas.

Words died in his throat as the defenders bowed their heads, resolution hardening their faces. Then Saad's voice cut through the dawn.

"Father!"

The spell took hold again. Vardon fell to all fours, unable to watch yet unable to block the sounds. His son's cries vibrated through the stones, through his bones, until they stopped with terrible suddenness.

When Vardon looked up, his vision swam red.

Below, the warrior-mages surged forward, halberds swinging in perfect unison. Vardon forced himself upright, mind calculating distances through the fog of grief.

Three hundred paces.

He raised his gauntleted hand. "First volley!"

A thousand arrows arced into the sky, dark against the dawn. They fell among the enemy ranks. Most glanced off magical wards, but some found flesh, dropping oxen and drawing inhuman howls.

Not enough. They need to be closer.

Two hundred paces now. The green glow of their weapons brightened as they approached, promising death to all behind the walls.

Vardon raised his hand again, grief hardening to purpose. They would pay in blood for every step toward his city.

Rika bolted upright, heart hammering against her ribs. Something had yanked her from sleep, a warning. Without hesitation, she sent her spirit slipping free of her body, searching for Queen Ellis. The royal chambers stood empty. Panic seized her.

A rooster crowed nearby, then squawked into silence. Guilt pricked her conscience as she followed the sound through the palace corridors, but she pressed on until the hallways erupted into frantic movement. Court-yards swarmed with people loading wagons, carrying belongings, herding bleating animals toward the river. Not chaos, this was Merric's work. Ordered evacuation in the face of certain doom.

Boats shuttled between the breached western wall and the northeast quay. Fragments of desperate conversation reached her: "King's at the East gate... can't hold them... take only essentials..."

Through the breach, she spotted Ellis standing on a makeshift dock. The queen remained statuesque despite the exhaustion etched in the lines of her face. Merric moved among the refugees, steadying them with quiet words and firm nods.

Rika drifted to Ellis and placed her spectral hands on the queen's shoulders. The intimacy made her hesitate. "Close your eyes," she whispered. "It's Rika."

The queen stiffened, then relaxed. Merric paused mid-gesture, frowned, then closed his eyes before redirecting a refugee who'd been approaching Ellis.

"A surge awakened me," Rika said, urgency threading her voice. "What's happened?"

Ellis's thoughts flowed back, steady but laced with grief: "The horde arrived at dawn. They executed Andreas and Saad before Vardon's eyes. Their numbers exceed two hundred thousand. If the trap at the East gate fails, they'll overrun us before sunset."

Cold dread pooled in Rika's stomach. The East gate, their last line of defense. "I'll get Shandar. We'll reinforce the gate."

"Don't tell Vardon," Ellis cautioned. "If he knew of extra defenses, he'd sacrifice himself and every remaining soldier."

"Understood." Rika withdrew, her spirit snapping back to her body with a jolt.

She raced to Shandar's bedside and shook the younger woman's shoulder. "Goat herder, wake up."

"Let me sleep," Shandar grumbled, burrowing deeper into her pillows.

"The city is falling," Rika hissed. "Now!"

Shandar's eyes snapped open, anger flashing before comprehension dawned. "What's happened?"

"Crenwelge is falling. We must fortify the East gate, quietly. The queen's orders. Vardon can't know."

Shandar's annoyance vanished, replaced by grim resolve. "Mother-rutting dung heap," she muttered, throwing off her blankets. Her voice cracked. "Does it ever get easier?"

"I fear it's only beginning." Rika handed her a steaming cup. "Drink. We'll need your strength."

"Should I tell Dagmar we're delayed?"

"I'll handle it."

Shandar's mouth quirked. "Rather face him than me? Don't hit your head on the doorframe telling him." The absurd humor grounded them both as battle cries echoed in the distance.

Rika rapped on Salem and Dagmar's door until the blanket inside shifted. Salem lay exposed, her hair-silk writhing over pale skin. Rika averted her eyes as Salem yanked the blanket up with a laugh.

"Crenwelge is falling," Rika said flatly. "We're reinforcing the gate. Be ready when we return. Will you tell Dagmar?"

"Passing that burden to me?" Salem's smile faded. "Go. Quickly."

Rika slipped through the predawn darkness back to camp, where Shandar waited, already armored.

"I've never been to Crenwelge," Shandar said, frowning. "How do I reinforce a gate I can't picture?"

The question struck at Rika's confidence. Another limitation of her gift.

"I was just there." She closed her eyes and shared the mental image: twin doors, sentinel tower, hidden seam. "You'll need to seal the halves, then bind a force-repellent protection."

Shandar tapped her lip. "What powers the shield?"

"There's an Aqua vein underground."

"No people in the channel this time," Shandar said, jaw tightening. "I've killed enough already."

The weight of those words hung between them as they clasped hands. Shandar's eyes held fierce determination and something softer, perhaps compassion for Rika's fear.

"Give me your hand," Rika whispered, and the world blurred.

They materialized beside the eastern gate. Bowstrings hummed overhead. Fireballs crashed against stone. Rika's spirit surged outward, tracing the faint pulse of power beneath them.

"There," she said. "Two steps south."

Shandar placed her palm to the earth and inhaled. Raw power coursed through her, Rika felt it roaring, heard it thrumming. Shame and awe tangled in her chest.

Is this what you always feel? she thought.

A mere taste, came Shandar's reply. Let's seal it.

Together they wove their magic: Rika's guidance directing Shandar's raw power. Aquamarine light lashed upward, reshaping stone into a seamless barrier.

Leave the outward face natural, Rika cautioned. No visible signs.

Shandar infused the hidden seam. The magic solidified, vanished.

Rebound spell? Shandar's question flickered in Rika's mind.

Water, Rika answered, and suddenly she was a child again, splashing in puddles, delighting in ripples expanding outward. Understanding bloomed between them as they wove the rebound charm. Aqua energy pulsed between gate and wall, then settled.

Anchor to the vein, Rika suggested. It must regenerate after each strike.

The magic curved like a river finding its path, feeding the shield continuously. Done, but would it hold against two hundred thousand?

They stepped back through the gate. In the distance, camp lights flickered as preparations continued. Rika met Shandar's gaze, both bearing the weight of what they'd witnessed, what was still to come.

"It won't be enough," Shandar whispered, voicing what neither wanted to admit.

"It has to be," Rika answered, watching the eastern sky lighten with false dawn. "Do you want to tell Ellis we let Vardon die?"

Flames blossomed on every arrowhead two hundred paces from the city wall. In an instant, a torrent of fire rained down on the writhing mass below.

King Vardon pressed his back against the cold stone, heart hammering. Guilt coiled in his gut like a serpent. Seven hundred and fifty seasons of peace, he'd believed it would last forever. What had he missed? What had driven this horde to his gates at last?

A vicious clang echoed as the first volley struck an invisible dome of crackling energy. Enemy mages wove the barrier above their ranks, and the firestorm rebounded into the sky. One lone arrow sailed past the shield, landing with a dull thud behind the horde. Undeterred, the monsters surged forward.

From the tower parapet, green fireballs spat overhead. Most fizzled out of range; a few landed with muted booms. The archers held their formation, two rotating rows, feeding arrow after arrow into the inferno until a living wall of flame barred their advance.

Vardon's stomach knotted as creatures, hulking beasts with singed fur, pressed on, flaming arrows lodging in flesh. Then he spotted it: a massive emerald sphere, arcing straight at the eastern rampart. Horror clenched his chest, here was no stopping it.

The explosion detonated twenty men in an instant. Their bodies vanished in a spray of blood and bone. Survivors stared, mouths agape, at gashes in the wall where comrades had been.

Retreat. The thought rose unbidden, and he crushed it. His right flank unleashed arrow after arrow, discipline reborn through desperation.

One shaft slewed through the eye-slit of an enemy mage. The man convulsed, then his death-cries detonated the left-side trap. Shockwaves rippled outward, dirt and flesh scattered like shredded cloth. Two lead mages, horses and all, disappeared in a single, thunderous blast.

The air barrier wavered. At last the front ranks were pinned in a spiky hedge of arrows.

But the reprieve was brief. Six enemy mages glowed with unholy power, weaving a fireball so huge the mounts beneath them seemed tiny. It hurtled into the gate's center.

A blinding wall of aquamarine flame roared outward. The green sphere shattered against it, its wrath rebounding into the horde. Sickly fire lanced through bodies, severing legs from torsos. Horses reared in agony, thundered, then collapsed in steaming heaps. Screams shredded the dawn air. Mages who'd launched the spell scattered, some crushed beneath their own mounts. For three hundred paces around the gate, everything writhed and died.

The slaughter silenced the archers' chant. Trained sequence gave way to primal fear. First they shot the injured horses to still their whinnies, then hesitated. Finally, they forced themselves back into the ritual: nock, flame, step forward, release, step back, over and over.

Vardon gripped the parapet as a rope snaked over the battlement. An archer clambered over, torch in hand. Vardon lurched forward: the young man turning at the rope's end was Glorin, his son.

"Not Glorin…not both in one day," he whispered, dread freezing his voice.

Silence slammed into him. The archers had ceased their volley.

"Sites, protect him!" Vardon roared.

Several bowmen rose in unison, but an enemy mage, unscathed amid the carnage, hurled a fireball. Glorin twisted aside, yet the blast caught his hip, spinning him into the stones. He pitched forward, torch flying from his hand. He glanced back at his father, hope glittering in his eyes, before a second sphere creamed him into nothing.

Six arrows leapt from bows, pinning the mage to a broken warhorse. But Vardon heard none of it. Guilt hollowed his chest as the torch clattered to the ground, sparking a tuft of grass.

A thunderous chain of explosions ignited when the right-side trap's fuse reached its end. Bodies and earth rocketed skyward, raining ruined flesh over the horde. The creatures recoiled, then turned tail and fled beyond arrow range.

Vardon forced himself to survey the devastation. Tremendous, yet folly against two hundred thousand monsters. The right column, having suffered least, had surged closest before Glorin's sacrifice. Now a third of them lay in shredded fragments drifting downriver. The rest regrouped instantly, swallowed by the oncoming tide.

He felt those final detonations echo inside him: Retreat now or lose everything. I can save the city.

He almost collapsed against the wind-tossed parapet, face slick with sweat and grief. Around him, hollow-eyed archers nibbled dry bread, bows idly resting on laps. The horde lingered five hundred paces out, just beyond reach, like a dark stain on the horizon.

Vardon's gaze found the jagged hole where the eastern wall had stood, red seeping into cracked stone. My sons...

He slunk into the tower's shadow and murmured a broken prayer to Lashnar, begging protection for those still alive. Then he crept to the narrow view-slit and watched the horde, motionless but not defeated.

Decision crystallized in his mind, as unstoppable as the tide. Teeth gritted, he stepped out onto the wall and spoke the order no king wants to give:

"Boats!"

Instantly, half his men sprang to their feet and raced for the eastern stairs, armor clinking like falling coins. They charged down toward the river and the fragile hope of Crenwelge's survivors.

Vardon watched them go, then faced the hellscape before his battered city. The other archers stayed, bows drawn but useless. The enemy mass waited beyond range, barely thinner for the carnage.

Five hundred paces out, Nudzh stood like a living statue between two wagons, charred arms of past victims dangling from his belt. His reptilian eyes glowed with terrible patience.

He waited. Not advancing, not retreating, only savoring the moment.

Vardon's blood ran ice. The true nightmare was only beginning.

Dawn broke over the Aster Hills, painting the refugee column in merciless light. Children trudged forward, eyes red-rimmed, faces hollow with exhaustion. The smallest ones huddled in wagons, clutching worn toys with white-knuckled fingers. A girl no older than five pressed a one-eyed doll to her chest, whispering promises of safety it couldn't understand.

Fifty knights circled the column, their armor catching the sun. Each rider scanned the horizon, hands never straying far from sword hilts. Their formation spoke what words didn't: these children would reach Tiereny, or the knights would die trying.

Behind the children came the supply wagons, women walking alongside with faces carved from stone. They gripped their cloaks against the morning chill, watching shadows with wary eyes. The promised vanguard of twelve thousand cavalry was nowhere to be seen.

Silence ruled the exodus. Only the creak of wheels and occasional shout from drivers broke the quiet. Between these refugees and Crenwelge stretched leagues of open road, a gauntlet they had no choice but to run.

At the river crossing, Queen Ellis watched the final evacuees with narrowed eyes. Her crown sat like a weight, simple black metal against dark braids. Beside her, Merric lunged toward four laborers struggling with a heavy crate suspended between poles.

"Steady!" He caught the wavering pole with one hand, the stumbling bearer with the other. The crate, a moment from plunging into the churning water, stabilized.

Ellis's mouth twitched, almost a smile. "Do they know death is on the other side?" she murmured. "This isn't a summer trip back home."

A young woman approached, curtseying awkwardly. "Majesty, the last wine barrel won't fit. What should..." She flinched at Ellis's expression.

"Lay it on its side. Lash it down." Ellis's voice cracked like ice. "Now go."

The woman fled. Merric squeezed Ellis's shoulder.

"She's frightened, El. They all are."

Ellis kicked a rock into the river. "It's just so simple."

"Nothing's simple when your world's ending." He studied her face. "I know you're worried for Vardon, but…"

"She's a wagonwright's daughter, Merric. Loading cargo is what she does."

"And today she's watching her life burn. Be their queen, not their taskmaster."

Ellis's cheeks colored. Before she could respond, Merric stiffened, eyes locking on something beyond her shoulder.

"TIME!" he shouted, bolting toward the bridge.

Ellis spun. Fire arrows arced against the sky, trailing smoke as they plummeted toward the castle. Merric was already halfway across the bridge, fingers finding the hidden trail of black powder she'd watched him lay three nights before.

Heart hammering, Ellis turned toward the waiting wagons, eyes searching the battlements for any sign of Vardon.

The first explosion shook the ground. People scattered toward the bridge as a second blast rocked the castle foundations. Merric dropped to his knees at the bridge's edge, checking that the powder line remained intact, their final defense when the moment came.

Miles away, on Crenwelge's far side, a rider in blood-red robes emerged from the river mist. He approached a massive figure waiting before the smoldering remnants of the morning's explosion.

"Shotoa." Nudzh's voice rumbled like granite sliding down a mountainside. "You failed to foresee their trap. I should melt you where you stand."

The mage bowed low from his saddle. Even bent, his eyes never left the monster's face.

"Chief mage replaceable," Nudzh warned.

"Ancient magics," Shotoa replied, his accent twisting the words into something older than human speech. "Dwarven craft, long forgotten by men. The oversight will not repeat." He straightened. "Found the vein that powers their gate. One strike there", he pointed, "and their defenses fall."

Six warrior mages formed a semicircle before them, hands weaving light into shields. "These will turn their arrows," Shotoa said.

"The rest of the city?"

"Empty. They've fled through a breach in the western wall. Only the archers remain." Shotoa's lips curled. "The last desperate defense of a dying kingdom."

Nudzh pulled his battle ax from the wagon beside him. The curved blade caught the sun, its edge hungry for blood. He turned toward Crenwelge, the mages scrambling to position themselves before him.

The first arrows fell short. The second volley struck the magical barrier and bounced away harmlessly. Nudzh never broke stride, each footfall bringing him closer to the doomed walls, each step measured and inevitable as death itself.

CHAPTER 19

GATHERING SHADOWS

A leaden sky hung over the forest, neither bright enough to comfort nor dark enough to threaten. Wind whispered through the trees, turning leaves inside out to reveal their pale undersides a restless, smoky dance against the colorless backdrop. Kumar led them northeast toward a narrow rift between twin hills, their destination a plateau where they would make camp for the night.

Blair's company fell into natural formation as they rode single file along the barely visible path. Two days after leaving the Mound, anticipation hummed among them. Finrod had convinced them all: the stones they sought waited in the dragon's lair, and despite the growing darkness in the world, their quest still had purpose.

The memory of last night's heated exchange still lingered in Blair's mind. Dagmar had been restless around the campfire, constantly rearranging firewood, his back pressed against the stone ring as if seeking its solidity.

"Once we've crossed the Squat Mountains at Furman's pass, we face the Waste." Dagmar had shifted, uncomfortable with his own words. "That's a devil's place even without evil hunting you through it." His eyes had grown distant. "Three-quarters of a moon to reach the mountains, if we're lucky."

Shandar had cut in sharply. "That's not possible. Triangul is almost full in the predawn sky. How much time do we actually have?"

Dagmar's arms had crossed, neck cords tightening. "I suppose you have a faster way?"

Shandar had risen, muscles coiled like a spring. "We will find a way. When I collaborate with the others, a path will be formed." She had deliberately positioned herself to block Dagmar's view of the others.

Dagmar stood then, bringing them face to face. "You will end reality if you go too far."

"You want to die," Shandar had hissed, flames beginning to lick along her forearms. "What do you care?"

The fire had intensified around Shandar's frame when Rika's scream cut through the tension. All eyes turned to find her rolling up her sleeves with deliberate calm.

"Shandar, Mistress of Fire," Rika had begun with exaggerated formality before her voice sharpened with scorn. "You want to attack one of our members? He's on our side. Be gentle." She hadn't missed Dagmar's raised eyebrow and tilted head. "And you, Master Dagmar, are a mercenary, a hired soldier. You will be commanded what to do. We paid your price."

Dagmar's fists had clenched at his sides, knuckles whitening. For a heartbeat, everyone froze, watching for his reaction. His eyes had burned, but Rika stood unwavering, though Blair had caught the momentary flicker of regret in her expression. She knew her bluntness was necessary to establish command, even as she hoped Dagmar would understand.

Salem had pulled him away from camp, and they hadn't returned until morning. Now Dagmar rode quietly, acceptance or at least resignation clear in his posture.

The company climbed the rift in single file: Kumar, Rika, Baltan, Rasslow, Shandar, Blair, Salem, Finrod, Arbor, and Dagmar. Pine and poplar surrounded them as they wove between fallen trunks and saplings, reaching for light.

The first explosion came without warning.

Pop-pop-POP!

A heartbeat of silence followed, then the ominous creak of splintering wood. Trees toppled around them. To Shandar's left, bark sprayed in a deadly arc as a massive pine crashed down, blocking her path. Her horse Sprite reared in pain and terror, bolting up the right slope. Shandar wrapped her arms around the animal's neck, barely keeping her seat as they galloped upward.

Time slowed for Blair as trees crashed on either side of him, missing Rika by inches. Another trunk slammed down before him, cutting off his path to the others ahead. Behind Dagmar, a wall of fallen timber sealed off their retreat. He watched Dagmar veer left up a gentler incline, only to be met by a hail of arrows, stones, and charging Northmen.

With fluid grace belying his age, Dagmar's sword flashed out, deflecting projectiles midair. He executed a backward roll off his horse's rump, slapping its flank to drive the animal into the attackers. In the moment of confusion that followed, his blade found three throats in rapid succession. Turning back toward his companions, Dagmar's expression shifted from determination to alarm as he saw Salem, Finrod, and Arbor approaching. Too late, he sensed movement behind him. As he pivoted, a blast of sickly green magic caught him square in the chest, hurling him toward his friends. He landed facedown and motionless, dust settling around his still form.

Baltan's world spun at the first explosions. Turning to check on Shandar. He registered their escape route, collapsing behind Dagmar, then saw splinters erupt from Sprite's flank. The horse bucked wildly with Shandar clinging desperately to its neck. Baltan turned his mount toward her, but Rasslow's iron grip seized his bridle.

"Blair has her," Rasslow said with unnerving certainty. "Rika is our duty now."

Baltan hesitated, then turned back just as a massive trunk crashed where he would have been moments before. Heart hammering, he urged his horse toward Rika. More trees fell on either side, creating a corridor that forced them upward toward the plateau. As they neared Rika, he caught Rasslow's eye and mouthed trap. Rasslow nodded grimly: trap.

They scanned the slope for Kumar, finding him halfway up with his horse, Dandy skidding on loose rock. Kumar waved frantically for Rika to advance while she shook her head, hands gesturing refusal. Her eyes had seen what awaited them. Baltan and Rasslow flanked her, hemming her in.

"It's a trap!" Rika shouted, her normally composed voice edged with panic. "They're waiting for us!"

"We know," Baltan said grimly. "They're splitting us up. No choice." They pressed closer, forcing her horse forward. "It must be sprung. There's nowhere else to go. Be ready, be smart."

Baltan whispered a desperate prayer to Lashnar, but no divine intervention came. At the plateau's edge, twenty Northmen and a warrior mage in crimson robes awaited them. Hope withered in Baltan's chest. Kumar halted, slowly raising his hands. Rasslow surveyed the forces arrayed against them, then followed suit. The trap had closed.

When mortal danger strikes, time seems to slow, allowing the mind to process what the body cannot yet accept. Blair experienced this distortion as trees crashed around him, some toward Rika, one blocking his path forward, multiple rows sealing off the retreat behind Dagmar.

Then reality crashed back at full speed.

Shandar.

The thought eclipsed all others. She was in danger, her horse bolting up the slope. Without hesitation, Blair wheeled his mount and spurred it after her, leaving the others to their fates.

In Crenwelge, the second half of the Archers executed their defensive dance along the wall. Every other man headed the long way, shooting as they passed each parapet to keep the illusion of full strength. Their arrows fell short or bounced harmlessly off the magical barrier surrounding the advancing Nudzh.

King Vardon followed the first of the second wave, staggering down the long corridor toward the eastern side of the castle grounds where the boats awaited. Hearing the men behind him, he straightened his spine and steadied his gait. A king must never show weakness, especially in defeat.

Against the back wall behind the launch point, Vardon watched as men boarded and boats magically reappeared at the tributary's start. Two handlers worked frantically, using poles to keep twenty vessels ready for the escaping archers. Sholin had created this transportation magic hundreds of seasons ago, and it had worked flawlessly since. Just beyond the dock, each boat disappeared into the wall, returning to the downslope where Vardon stood.

He marveled at Queen Ellis's resourcefulness at finding twenty boats so quickly. Usually, they kept only three, but to evacuate a thousand men, twenty were essential. The evacuation area teemed with archers waiting their turn. Merric's organizational scheme had proven invaluable.

"Like those oilcloths we use on saddles," Merric had explained. "You fold them back and forth to make them smaller for storing. Same with archers zigzag them in a single line, always moving."

Vardon estimated about a hundred men remained, each facing a six-minute journey through the wall. As the second wave appeared, he called out, "Archer, where was the monster when you left?"

"Three hundred paces and gaining, Your Majesty," came the reply. "He's a big brute with a stride to match."

Vardon bowed his head momentarily. I lost both my eldest sons today, and I still don't know why. Pushing aside his grief, he assessed the situation. Boats were stacking up behind the boarding dock until they were departing faster than new ones could be loaded. This required his personal attention.

Drawing himself to full height, Vardon's voice rang against the stone walls. "Stay focused! Five hundred of your comrades are counting on you to see tomorrow." He planted his hands on his hips, every inch the king despite his exhaustion. "Know your row when boarding. Hold your bow, quiver, and sword between your legs. Count off in fives. Nudzh will attack soon; we must be gone before then. Other people's lives depend on you."

His commanding presence had the desired effect. The count rang out, and each man prepared his gear for quick boarding. The next two boats left smoothly, though a stumble nearly created chaos with the third. A quick hand steadied the falling archer, and the evacuation continued. The line moved faster now, and Vardon felt a flicker of hope. They would all escape before the gate fell.

Then the ground heaved beneath them. A mighty blow reverberated through the stone, raising dust and triggering coughs. The archers continued boarding without pause, their discipline holding.

Vardon frowned. That hadn't felt like an attack on the gate or walls. It was deeper, as if the earth itself had been wounded. He needed to see for himself. After a quick count of the remaining men, he climbed the wall stairs, brushing aside the protests of archers who urged him to evacuate.

From the parapet, he confirmed the horde remained three hundred paces distant. Leaning over the battlements, he searched for Nudzh and found him returning from the eastern wall by the river's edge, his massive axe dripping with aqua-tinged liquid. In moments, the monster would reach the gate, and death would follow.

Turning to descend, Vardon stopped short. Seven archers stood waiting on the stairs, their faces grim with determination. They had disobeyed his order to evacuate, choosing instead to stand with their king until the end.

"Get out of here! That gate explodes at any moment. We must reach the boats before it does, or those mages will make us suffer." King Vardon's voice strained with urgency as he jabbed his finger toward the waiting vessels.

An archer stepped to the wall, nocked an arrow, and loosed it at Nudzh. The shaft struck true, piercing the monster's left eye.

A roar of agony shattered the air. Nudzh, half-blinded and enraged, slammed his battle axe against the eastern wall. The impact sent tremors through the stone foundation. Vardon and everyone near him crashed to the ground as the shockwave rippled outward.

The king knew they wouldn't move until he led the way. He pushed himself up, brushed dust from his royal garments with a quick sweep of his hands, and headed for the stairs. He took them two at a time, boots pounding the stone, his personal guard close behind.

At the bottom, he doubled over, hands on his knees, lungs burning. The waiting men stared at him, frozen in indecision.

"Get on the damn boats or die watching me breathe!" Vardon bellowed. "Move!"

The spell broke. Men surged forward, counting off as they boarded, each vessel filling and pulling away to make room for the next. As Vardon straightened, catching his breath, he turned to find seven archers still standing behind him, unwavering.

"Your Highness," one began, "the Queen spoke to us and..."

"Say no more." Vardon cut him off, a flicker of understanding crossing his face. "So, you're my personal guard. Fine. Go prepare our boat."

The ground heaved beneath them. Vardon crashed to the stone floor again as plaster and grout filled the air with choking dust. The shock rumbled through the castle, toppling everyone in its path and violently rocking the boats in the water. Men clung desperately to the gunwales to avoid being thrown overboard.

Outside, Nudzh stood before the gate, his massive form radiating fury. Blood streamed from his ruined left eye, which he held in one hand, still impaled on the arrow while his other fist clenched his mighty battle axe.

He positioned himself: axe raised high behind his back, hips thrust forward, knees bent. His mind focused, channeling his rage into the gleaming blade of his weapon. With a primal scream, he struck the gate dead center.

The impact sent him staggering backward as destructive energy tore outward in all directions. This shockwave, twice as powerful as the first, ripped through his own forces. Three hundred paces of death carved through the horde, tearing bodies apart from bottom to top. The stench of blood and entrails saturated the air before the gate.

Where Nudzh's blow had struck the ground, a vein in the earth had ruptured. The left and right flanks of his army, five hundred paces back, had been spared. They would be the ones to pour into the capital once the gate fell.

Nudzh climbed back to his feet and retrieved his axe. He suspended the agony of his wounded eye. There would be time for pain later. Veins bulged against his skin as muscles strained with effort. Spittle gathered at the corners of his mouth as he released a guttural roar.

"Willooow."

The sound echoed off the walls like a curse. Standing before the gate, he saw the green glow of his power clinging to the structure. Nudzh gathered his mental force, hesitated for one breath, then pressed his palm against the barrier.

The gate exploded inward, vaporizing into dust.

He turned to his commanders, his voice low with menace.

"Kill everyone you find and bring me the King's head."

The horde surged forward, pouring into Crenwelge.

Inside, Vardon dusted himself off and stumbled toward the dock. The explosion of the gate sent him reeling, his head ringing from the concussion. Through the disorientation, he noticed one of his seven personal guards organizing the final evacuation. The man was setting up a defensive line of twenty archers across the hall, being counted off in pairs.

"Ground to sky, every two men," the guard commanded. "Legs, heart, neck, and head. Shoot until your quiver is empty, then run to the last boat. Everybody's lives depend on it."

The man strode purposefully to the front line, knelt beside his comrades, and nocked an arrow. Looking up, he caught Vardon watching.

"Sire, it's pointless if you're here." He tilted his head toward the ceiling with a heavy sigh. "Move your ass!"

Vardon turned on his heel and climbed aboard the waiting boat. Looking back, he raised his voice in a final salute: "Crenwelge, our home!"

"Honor bestowed," the archers responded in unison, their voices steady despite the approaching doom.

The first of the Aloiene creatures appeared in the hall. Two steps in, it became a pin cushion of arrows. Vardon twisted to look downriver, amazed by how swiftly the current carried them away from the castle. From this distance, he could see the enemy wave a shoulder-to-shoulder mass that stepped over fallen comrades without pause.

His archers' quivers emptied quickly. They peeled away from the line, racing toward the boats. The unexpected length of the enemies' halberds caught many by surprise. Men fell, thinking themselves beyond reach. Suddenly, the light changed, drawing Vardon's attention to a massive hole blasted through the castle wall.

Through this new opening, Vardon spotted refugees hustling supplies across a makeshift bridge. As he watched, someone blew a clear, loud note on a horn. The civilians spotted him and abandoned their goods, fleeing across the bridge toward safety.

Without warning, a section of the bridge collapsed. A wagon, an ox, and two riders plunged into the churning river below. A bottleneck formed instantly panicked people trapped on the remaining span while the king's party approached rapidly from behind.

Merric, the royal gamekeeper, was already shouting orders before the wagon disappeared beneath the water's surface.

"Secure those rails over the breach!" His voice cut through the chaos, his brow furrowed in concentration. "They're all dead unless you succeed! Hold the beams like you're preparing for a log toss in basic training. Now slide to the edge and drop them across!"

The men struggled with the five-pace rails but bridged the gap. People streamed across the bottleneck slowly clearing. Vardon approached the damaged section but stopped, turning back toward the castle. He couldn't leave yet, not while his men still fought.

Merric was nearly pulling his hair out. "Your Majesty! Continue across!" When Vardon didn't move, Merric shooed the remaining civilians ahead, then glanced toward the wagons. As he turned to leave, he spotted Queen Ellis keeping her promise, riding away now that Vardon had escaped the castle.

Fighting against the flow of refugees, Merric pushed toward Vardon just as the first Aloiene creatures appeared from the hole in the wall. He grabbed the king by the shoulder and spun him around.

"We must leave now," Merric insisted. "Show your archers the way. Be an example. The king crosses first."

"But I left twenty archers behind," Vardon protested, his voice hollow. "Where are they?"

Merric's face hardened. "They gave their lives so you wouldn't have to. Now move!" He shoved Vardon forward.

Reluctantly, Vardon turned and headed for the bridge. Five archers remained on the castle side once he crossed, the monsters nearly upon them. The last archer miscalculated, a zag when a zig was needed, and fell to an Aloiene's reach. But as the creature stepped past, no longer considering the fallen man a threat, the archer pulled his blade from the dirt and sliced across the monster's legs, hamstringing it before he died.

His sacrifice bought precious seconds. The remaining men crossed, lit the fuse, and destroyed the bridge behind them.

Vardon, the last of his subjects now safely across, climbed the hill that led to the King's Road. At the crest, he looked back at his castle one last time.

A figure appeared from the hole in the wall: Shotoa, the enemy mage. Their eyes met across the distance. Without hesitation, Shotoa raised his arms and hurled sickly green fireballs toward the king.

Vardon stood frozen, unable to comprehend that death was rushing toward him. A royal guard leapt forward, shoving him aside. The magical fire struck the man squarely, dissolving him instantly into gray dust. A fragment of the spell grazed Vardon's hip, sending him crashing to the ground.

The four remaining archers of his personal guard fired on the mage. Merric dropped to Vardon's side, examining the wound where fabric had been torn away. Blood seeped from the king's hip.

Shotoa stepped aside, allowing more Aloiene to pour through the breach. One archer secured a horse while Merric tied off a makeshift bandage around the king's injury. As Vardon settled into the saddle, the farthest section of the bridge exploded, followed by a concussive blast that obliterated the rest of the span. A heartbeat later, they heard and felt another explosion the King's Road bridge collapsing, cutting off the monsters' pursuit.

Shotoa lay sprawled by the castle wall, injured but still moving. Merric and the archers scrambled to their feet and raced after Vardon as he rode up the hill to rejoin the refugees. Behind them, smoke rose from the ruins of Crenwelge, marking the end of an era.

CHAPTER 20

SEEDS OF HOPE

Vardon woke to pain and the rhythmic creak of wagon wheels. He kept his eyes closed, allowing reality to settle back into his fractured awareness. Each breath sent daggers through his side.

He opened his eyes to a riot of colors in a Zingari wagon, its interior a kaleidoscope of reds, blues, and golds that swam before his vision. Ellis slept in a chair beside his bunk, her head tilted at an uncomfortable angle. A strand of silver-streaked hair had fallen across her face. Even exhausted, even afraid, she was magnificent.

She shouldn't be here. She should lead their people, not watching him die.

Vardon reached toward his abdomen, fingers finding the bandaged wound. Heat radiated through the dressing unnatural, wrong, and he jerked his hand away with a sharp intake of breath.

Ellis startled awake, at once alert. She leaned forward, checked his bandages with practiced efficiency, then met his eyes. The crease between her brows told him everything.

"How far to Newburg?" Vardon forced a smile, as if they were discussing the weather.

"A day, perhaps a day and a half." Ellis's voice was hollow, her eyes bloodshot. The proud shoulders that had never bent under the weight of a crown now sagged with exhaustion.

"I've been unconscious for over a quarter moon." He inhaled deeply, wincing as fire lanced through his side. "What do they say about their king now?"

"That you're a great king." Ellis stared at her hands. "That we could do no better."

"I should raise taxes, then. Bring them back to their senses."

Ellis punched his arm lightly, a ghost of a smile crossing her lips. Vardon took deliberately measured breaths, fighting to appear stronger than he was. The crease returned to Ellis's brow.

"Come on, El." He squeezed her hand harder this time. "Quit stalling."

Ellis met his gaze, then looked away. "No one here knows this magic. Sho and Tartus have vanished. Their absence speaks volumes." Her voice dropped to a whisper. "Time is critical, Vardon. The people watch you with equal parts hope and desperation. The winds carry hints of an approaching storm." She paused. "Your only chance is if they reach you soon."

"That bad?" Vardon squeezed her hand again. "What's our status? Where's the Horde?"

"We lose people with every league." Ellis's voice turned clinical, her defense against despair. "Some simply walk away. Others..." She shook her head. "One man just knelt down, sat back on his heels, and died. We left him there. He wanted surrender, so we granted it."

Her neck bent, eyes fixed on something distant and terrible. "Even the priests are faltering. Two have disappeared fled, they say. As for the Horde, the last runner reported they've nearly repaired both bridges. Two days, and they'll march again."

She was always direct with him. No false comfort, no pleasant lies. He loved her for that.

Ellis hesitated, then added, "I haven't heard from Rika since Crenwelge fell. I pray they're safe and on course." She dabbed his forehead with a cool cloth.

A sharp knock rattled the back of the wagon before the tarp was thrust aside. Sunlight sliced into the dim interior.

"Your Majesties." A guard bowed. "Messenger from Newburg."

Behind him stood a boy sixteen at most in the dust-covered summer uniform of the King's Guard. His eyes darted nervously as he shifted from foot to foot.

"Get this man a drink and something to wash with," Ellis commanded, then addressed the messenger directly. "What you have to tell us is important, but ten moments won't make a difference. I won't have you bringing all that dust to your king."

Surprise flickered across the young man's face, blooming into a tentative smile. "It's true, then you really care about people."

"Was there doubt?" Ellis arched an eyebrow.

The messenger bowed and accepted a waterskin and towel from a guard. Ellis used those precious moments to help Vardon sit upright, wiping his face and straightening his clothes. By the time the young man returned, Vardon looked almost kingly again.

"I am Vardon Willow, King of Monde," he said, voice steady despite the pain. "And you are?"

The messenger swallowed hard, composing himself. "Your Majesty, I am Alain Knightswood, son of Commander Kaine Knightswood of the Newburg Guard." He straightened his shoulders. "May I deliver my message?"

Vardon nodded.

"Tartus and Sholin have arrived in Newburg," Alain reported. "They've gathered every ship from Newburg to Tiereny. They'll transport as many refugees as possible by water while the rest continue on foot." He looked down, unable to meet the king's eyes.

"That should ease the burden on our animals and increase our speed." Vardon's voice was steady, but his face betrayed him a flash of pain as he shifted position.

"Map," Ellis called sharply. A guard handed her a rolled parchment, which she spread across her lap. "The King's Road approaches the main gate and continues along the wall. Those boarding ships must skirt eastward to reach Sea Gate." Her fingers traced the route. "We'll prioritize children, the sick, and the elderly, then women, then men." She looked up sharply. "The wagons to transport them will be sorely missed. Is there transportation available within the city?"

Alain started, realizing the queen was addressing him directly. "The carriage and wagon guild would help for payment."

"Payment is not an issue." Color rose in Ellis's cheeks. "Are you telling me they aren't already preparing to evacuate the city?"

The young man shuffled his feet, tugging at his collar. "We didn't believe the reports, Your Majesty. Surely there's enough magic to counter this threat, at least, that's what my father thinks."

Ellis's jaw tightened. Before she could respond, Vardon spoke.

"Son, it's real." His voice carried the weight of his crown. "The kingdom has lost two major cities. I have lost my two eldest sons to this darkness."

Alain went still, mouth falling open.

"Death approaches," Vardon continued, his voice rising with each word. "The end of times is upon us. You can surrender to it or run with us to make our stand at Tiereny and pray Blair's quest succeed. We'll provide you a fresh horse ride back immediately and begin preparations."

Ellis cut in, her gaze intense and cold. "You will seek Sholin A'Tai and inform him he must appear before his king immediately." She leaned forward, finger stabbing the air for emphasis. "Tell no one I requested him. Do you swear?"

The young man paled, swaying slightly. Ellis gripped his shoulder to steady him. Her touch seemed to wake him from his shock. He stood taller, hand over heart, in salute.

"I swear, Your Majesty."

Alain hesitated, glancing around. "Might I take Stepper with me? He's my horse. I've had him since I was five. He has the stamina for this task, but I won't refuse a fresh mount if offered." His smile came too quickly, trying to mask the fear in his eyes.

"Stepper will await your return," Ellis said firmly. "Complete your task, then come back to claim him."

Alain bowed and left. Through the open wagon flap, Vardon watched the young man mount a horse the guards had brought around. The boy rode off in a cloud of dust, carrying the weight of a dying kingdom's last hope.

Vardon closed his eyes, the pain in his side nothing compared to the burning question in his mind: would Blair succeed where he had failed?

Silence settled over the forest, broken only by the diminishing crunch of retreating footsteps as the Northmen and Wizards vanished among the trees. Arbor knelt beside Dagmar's motionless form, gently rolling him away from the trunk where he'd been thrown. His fingers pressed against Dagmar's neck, searching for a pulse.

Salem appeared at his side, her silver eyes unnaturally calm. "Is he dead?" she asked, leaning close.

Arbor's gaze flickered to her face. "No. Unconscious." His frown deepened. "You don't seem concerned."

"He plans to die on this journey." Salem's voice carried ancient resignation. "Though I expected something more... grand. Not this early skirmish." She reached toward Dagmar's temple, her fingers hovering inches from his skin. The connection between them forged over a millennium of shared existence, hummed like a plucked string.

"Step back," Arbor warned, rising quickly. "He might wake fighting."

They retreated as Dagmar's body tensed. His eyes snapped open, immediately finding Salem's face.

"I take it we didn't win," he said. The tension drained from his body as he sank deeper against the earth.

"There are just the four of us," Arbor replied. "The others are gone. For now, the area is clear of enemies."

Finrod appeared from the shadows as if summoned, his elvish features tight with barely contained fury. He knelt, examined Dagmar with a healer's practiced eye, then rose to his full height.

"Weren't we supposed to be under the forest's protection?" Finrod's voice dropped to a dangerous whisper. "You assured us the wards extended to the pass."

Dagmar pushed himself upright, back braced against the tree. "Magic lives. It shifts." He drew a deep breath and expelled it forcefully. "They knew our route, our destination, our timing. That knowledge requires proximity."

The accusation hung in the air between them. Each retreated into silence, exploring private suspicions. Finrod's head cocked, a muscle in his jaw twitching. Arbor stiffened, arms crossing as he moved to stand beside his mount. Salem closed her eyes, head bowed, lips pressed into a bloodless line. Dagmar pinched the bridge of his nose, controlling his breathing with deliberate care.

"Arbor," Finrod finally said, "track them. Find where they went. We'll make camp nearby, not here, exactly. Time is precious."

Arbor nodded once and disappeared into the forest. The others began assembling a small camp, each movement precise and wary.

The sliver of wood protruding from Sprite's chest remained invisible to Shandar as the mare reared backward. Hooves slipped on loose stones, haunches hit dirt, then the horse lunged upward with explosive force. Curses erupted from their companions, but Shandar couldn't spare attention as she fought to stay mounted. From stumble to full gallop up a slope, no sane rider would attempt all in a heartbeat. Shandar threw herself forward, grasping for the bridle but finding only the horse's neck. She slid backward, fingers desperately clutching the saddle's cantle.

Sprite burst between two pines onto a tiny natural platform and halted, sides heaving. Shandar dismounted on shaking legs and secured the reins to a tree. Below, Blair zigzagged upward, coaxing his reluctant mount across the treacherous incline.

Memory flooded back: explosions, falling trees, being cut off from the others, Sprite's panic. She examined the horse and found the cause, a three-inch splinter of pine embedded in her chest. Shandar pulled it free, wishing she could heal the wound.

A spark ignited at her fingertips. Fire bloomed around the injury, then vanished, taking the wound with it. Gooseflesh rippled across her arms.

"I can heal," she whispered, staring at her palms.

"Heal what?" Blair asked, his voice soft with wonder.

Shandar spun toward him, flames erupting around her body in a protective cocoon.

Blair stepped back. "Whoa, Mistress! Didn't mean to startle you."

Shandar inhaled deeply, held the breath, then released it slowly through her nose. The fire receded.

"I'm not all right," she said, voice tight. "I was attacked, and I ran. Some Mistress of Fire I am can't control my horse, let alone defeat evil." She stepped forward, fingers brushing the chain at Blair's neck. His hand found her back, steadying her.

"The horse acted on instinct," he said. "Not your fault... Mistress."

Shandar's gaze hardened. She loved him, that's why he still breathed, but her face revealed nothing. She remembered the day Blair and Kumar arrived with Rika, how everyone warned against pursuing Rika. She'd let them believe that's what she'd done.

"What happened?" she asked, shoulders slumping with exhaustion.

"We were attacked and separated. Four ahead, us here, four behind. That's all I know." Blair glanced at the darkening sky. "The forest's protection should have extended to the pass. Barriers are failing. We need to move faster. Time is running out."

"What now?"

"Back down. Find the trail. With luck, we'll meet Finrod on the way."

Shandar closed her eyes, head resting against the mountainside. Since her magic awakened, her perception had expanded. If she concentrated, she could sense Blair's gaze on her, feel his smile. Warmth spread through her, bringing an involuntary blush. She sat up abruptly, shielding herself from his perception.

Blair, kneeling beside her, startled at her sudden movement. "Bad dream?"

"Was I asleep? How long?"

"Just a moment. We should start down. I'll lead."

"No. I got us up here. It's my responsibility to get us back."

"A good commander knows when to delegate," Blair said. "I've spent two seasons on my own in wilderness like this."

"So, I'm a commander now? Not just a little girl playing with fire?"

"I've never called you a little girl," Blair whispered.

Shandar closed her eyes, anger flaring inward. Why did I say that? That's how I feel, not what he said. Her cheeks burned with a different heat of embarrassment.

Blair scanned the steep trail, searching for the safest descent, when Sprite's sharp whinny pulled his attention back. Shandar sat hunched in her saddle, her entire body convulsing with violent tremors. He reached her in three strides, easing her from the horse to the ground. She curled inward, arms wrapped around herself, rocking and shivering uncontrollably.

He cradled her head between his hands and gently kissed her closed eyelids. Then, with deliberate slowness, he lowered his mouth to hers and kissed her deep. Time seemed to suspend itself. Her trembling ceased as she returned the kiss.

When he pulled away, her eyes were clear, fingers tracing her lips in wonder.

"Are you okay?" he whispered.

"Someday I will be." A small smile formed on her lips as she rose and remounted Sprite. "Are you all right?"

Blair nodded, something shifting between them as they began their descent into shadow.

Atop a small knoll, the prisoners' tent stood isolated against the darkening sky. Inside, Rika's wrists chafed against the ropes binding her hands behind her back, her ankles similarly bound. She leaned against the canvas wall, exchanging glances with Baltan and Kumar. Where had they taken Rasslow?

A narrow slit in the tent flap offered a view of the encampment. Scattered fires dotted the landscape, illuminating haphazardly pitched tents as though the army had simply stopped marching and made camp wherever they stood. At the center blazed the major fire where warrior mages had gathered, their gestures sharp with fury. Though Rika couldn't understand their words, their tone carried clearly: rage, impatience, purpose.

"We need to understand what's happening before we act," she whispered, keeping her voice low enough that only her companions could hear.

Rika inched forward on her knees, then dropped to her stomach near the opening. With practiced movements, she drew her knees to her chest and worked her bound hands beneath her body until they were in front. The minor victory made her breath catch. At least now she could defend herself if needed.

Through the gap, the scene revealed itself more clearly. The warrior mages treated the Northmen with casual cruelty that made her stomach clench. Five paces away, a mage flicked his hand in a whipping motion. A welt appeared instantly across a Northman's face as he turned away from the blow, not even raising a hand in defense. The Northmen's eyes were hollow, devoid of resistance or hope. They had accepted their subjugation completely.

Most curious of all, no guards stood watch at their tent. Either their captors were foolishly overconfident, or something more calculated was at play.

Emboldened, Rika widened the opening slightly. No shouts of alarm came. No rough hands pushed her back. She adjusted the flap further, scanning the entire camp.

Her heart stopped.

There sat Rasslow on a log beneath a distant tree, completely unbound. A Northman approached him, head bowed, dropping a plate of food at his feet and offering a steaming mug. Rasslow took it without acknowledgment, like a lord accepting his due.

Rika jerked back, bile rising in her throat. Her hands trembled as she turned away.

"Kumar," she called softly, lifting her chin to mask her shock. "Could you come here, please?"

Kumar rolled toward her with the fluid grace of an elven warrior. His hands already worked free. He leaned close, his breath warm against her ear.

"Look to your left," she whispered. "Past the tent and tree, to the log beneath it. Tell me what you see."

While Kumar investigated, Rika moved to Baltan and worked at his ankle bindings. His face crinkled with unasked questions, but she shook her head slightly. Confirmation first, then discussion.

Kumar returned moments later, all traces of restraint gone from his limbs. His face had hardened to stone.

"He's being treated as a mercenary," Kumar whispered, "not as a prisoner."

Together they freed Baltan, then directed him to look. When he returned, his face had soured, but uncertainty still lingered in his eyes.

"It doesn't look good," Baltan admitted, shoulders slumping. "But we don't know everything. Perhaps he's playing along to gather information?" His voice rose at the end, pleading. "Don't you agree we should give him the benefit of doubt?"

Rika and Kumar exchanged glances, arms crossed over their chests, expressions flat.

"No," Rika said softly. "I don't."

The mountain ledge offered just enough space for the horses and riders to rest, though the animals shifted nervously, sensing the steep drop merely a pace away. The wind carried the scent of snow from higher peaks.

As they prepared a meager meal, Dagmar began muttering, his agitation growing with each passing moment. The hair at his nape bristled like a threatened hound's.

Finrod reached over, tapping Dagmar's shoulder. "What troubles you?"

Dagmar sprang to his feet, pacing the narrow ledge. "The covenant," he said, voice rising. "How can it not be standing? It was meant to last forever!" His face blanched as he stepped backward. "What happened to the covenant? This can't be possible!"

Finrod stared, taken aback by the outburst. "What covenant?"

The question brought Dagmar to his knees, a sound like a wounded animal escaping his throat. Salem moved swiftly to his side, placing a calming hand on his head. Under her touch, Dagmar's breathing steadied, though his eyes remained wild.

"The Talon Covenant," Dagmar explained, fingers restlessly working the back of his neck. "An agreement arranged by the mage Tartarus, allowing humans to govern all of Monde except the lands north of Talon Pass."

He rose to his feet, standing before Finrod with the gravity of history in his stance.

"It revived Lashnar's calling, guiding humans toward contentment through magic. The covenant erased all memory of mythical creatures from human minds: dragons, elves, fairies, leaving no trace that could ever be recovered."

Dagmar couldn't remain still. His hands punctuated each word, his body swaying with the weight of revelation.

"The covenant wove an enchantment of tranquility into the Ceremony of Making itself. Not to make humans complacent, but to diminish their hunger for rapid advancement, encouraging them to appreciate the present rather than constantly reaching for more."

His eyes found Finrod's. "You passed through the barrier on your way down, did you not?"

Finrod's bark of laughter answered clearly.

"A conclave was held at what is now called Homested," Dagmar continued, his voice dropping to a reverent hush. "Every leader of the magical races signed: Elves, Dwarves, Fairies, Trolls, Giants, Dragons, Elementals, and Wraiths." His expression darkened. "Demons, Goblins, and humans never knew of the covenant. They never signed."

Salem's eyes met Finrod's over Dagmar's shoulder. The unspoken question hung between them: If the covenant had fallen, what ancient protections had fallen with it?

The wind strengthened as the royal caravan approached the sea, carrying the scent of salt and coming rain. Inside the covered wagon, Queen Ellis refused to roll up the canvas sides despite the stifling air. The people needed reassurance, not the sight of their dying king.

She silently cursed Sholin for his absence. Where was he when they needed him most?

The wagon's interior had grown stale. If she allowed herself to notice, Ellis could detect the faint odor of rot beneath the herbal poultices. She considered opening just one side for fresh air, then dismissed the thought. A strand of hair fell across her forehead; she pushed it back with uncharacteristic anger, suddenly aware she couldn't remember when she had last bathed.

King Vardon's head shifted on the pillow. Ellis looked at her husband, her throat tightening. His skin had taken on the waxy pallor of approaching death. She dipped a cloth in cool water and gently wiped his face, her touch lingering on the familiar contours now growing sharp with illness.

Memory swept her away without warning.

She was seventeen again, sitting alone at the center table in Crenwelge's grand banquet hall, overwhelmed by its vastness. Hundreds of unlit candles waited in their sconces. Tapestries larger than her entire bedroom hung from the walls. Merric, her family friend and honorary big brother, had brought her to see the palace after being named the king's huntsman. He'd left her "just for a moment" while securing his position with the quartermaster.

Ellis gazed at the empty dance floor, imagining herself waltzing with a handsome prince, when a hand settled on her shoulder. Assuming it was Merric returned, she spun around, words of reproach ready on her lips.

"You left me here all alone and you've been gone..." The words died as she faced a stranger. Instinct and indignation took over. She stepped on his foot, swept his legs from beneath him, and drove her knee into his head before she could think.

Merric rushed in, took in the scene, and smiled. He extended a hand to the young man sprawled on the floor.

"I warned you she could be a handful if you weren't polite," Merric said, helping him up. "What did you do? Touch her?"

The stranger rubbed his jaw, wincing. "She seemed lost in thought. I only touched her shoulder to announce myself." He managed a rueful laugh. "Next I knew, I was on the floor with my bell nearly rung."

Ellis's mortification turned to anger as they laughed together, ignoring her. She tapped her foot impatiently.

Merric finally turned to her, eyes dancing with mischief. "Ellis Whyte, may I introduce Prince Vardon Willow, our next king."

Present-day Ellis smiled at the memory. Vardon had never let her forget it, teasing her whenever she pouted. "Perhaps I should tell the court how you manhandled the prince," he would whisper, making her laugh despite herself.

A soft laugh escaped her lips now, just as the wagon lurched to a halt.

"Riders approaching, Your Highness," came a voice, accompanied by a tapping at the rear of the wagon.

Ellis glanced at Vardon. He slept or seemed to, which was for the best. She stood, futilely attempting to smooth her crumpled dress. After a quick check in her hand mirror and an adjustment of stray hairs, she moved to the back of the wagon. She pushed aside the flaps and stepped onto the stool placed by the attendant.

Through the gathering dusk, she recognized Sholin A'Tai on his black mare with golden eyes. His shoulder-length white hair fluttered behind him as he rode, the silver quarter moon and star emblem gleaming on his breast, the mark of his magical credentials. His lean frame appeared unchanged by the years, as tireless as ever. Behind him rode Alain, the commander's son. Ellis relaxed slightly. Perhaps Alain had kept his word and remained silent about the king's condition.

She pointed to a man walking beside another wagon. "Sir, would you ensure the caravan continues into the city? We'll catch up shortly."

The man froze, wide-eyed, then swallowed and bowed deeply. "Yes, Your Majesty." He smiled, hurrying back to his position.

"Keep moving," he called to the others. "Nothing to see here."

Ellis suppressed a smile, always surprised by how a simple courtesy and clear direction could inspire such eager service.

She noticed Alain approaching and halted him with an outstretched palm. "Your horse is at the rear of the caravan. Retrieve it and return. I can see in Sholin's eyes that he needs you here, but not yet."

Alain stopped abruptly, bowed without speaking, and hurried away.

As Sholin dismounted and approached, Ellis stepped behind the wagon, away from curious eyes. When he reached her, she embraced him fiercely, releasing the tension she'd carried in her shoulders for days.

"It's bad," she whispered into his shoulder, her voice muffled enough that no one could overhear. "I don't think he can be saved, but I need you to tell me for certain."

Sholin returned her embrace, offering comfort through his strength. "Your Majesty, I will do everything in my power. We will save him."

Ellis felt his reluctance as he released her and moved toward the wagon. This was the curse of his unnaturally long life watching friends wither while he remained unchanged. She watched as Sholin steeled himself, pushed aside the canvas flap, and climbed inside to sit beside the king.

Her king. Her Vardon. The man who had changed everything.

He observed the corruption spreading from his leg, snaking through his veins, and consuming his entire body. It was devouring him slowly, and it must have been painful. Sho placed his hand on Vardon's forehead, numbing the pain in his mind. The pain persisted, but Vardon was no longer aware of it. Vardon opened his eyes and smiled at his friend.

"You've blocked the pain. I can think clearly again, thank you. Does she know I'm dying?"

Sholin squeezed his hand and replied, "She knows."

A covered wagon stood just beyond the firelight of the prisoners' camp, its weathered canvas glowing amber against the darkness. Rasslow stared at it, bile rising in his throat. He had stood in that same wagon weeks ago, outside the walls of Newburg, fresh from his Ceremony of Making. The memory soured in his mind: his father's desperate confession about owing money to every lender in the city, the weight of family survival suddenly thrust upon Rasslow's shoulders.

The interior had surprised him then exquisite craftsmanship in every detail. Handcrafted planks formed walls nine paces long and two wide. Drawers and compartments nested within each other with mathematical precision. A silk-cushioned settee curved along one wall, its leather pillows inviting despite the circumstances. Four large spoked wheels supported the structure, while a stovepipe curled over the white-tarped roof.

The wagon door swung open. Galon Valdove came out first, tall and unnaturally thin, as if his skin had been stretched over too little flesh. His pockmarked oval face centered on a bulbous nose that twitched constantly. Behind him followed his servant, Moirae Fate, an Underworld nymph barely reaching a man's thigh in height. Her pure white hair curled at the tips, giving the impression of horns an effect she enhanced by painting certain strands black. Her floor-length black gown seemed unnaturally still as she moved, a silver-meshed brooch catching the firelight as it held her hooded cape in place.

Galon's lips curled into what might have been a smile. "Well, Master Langdon, your obligation is almost met. The Mages require more now that you're here." His nose wrinkled. "Where is the Mistress?"

"Almost met?" Rasslow's voice climbed an octave. "I've done exactly what you demanded back in Newburg. My obligation is fulfilled!" His hands balled into fists at his sides.

Galon stepped closer, his breath smelling of decay. "Do you see the Mistress in our possession? I think not." He tapped Rasslow's chest with one bony finger. "Deliver her to me, and everything will be..." his lips stretched wider, "... right as rain."

"Are you blind?" Rasslow's jaw tightened as he fought to control his voice. "I was captured with the others and separated from my party. I'm as trapped here as the Northmen." His fingers trembled against his thighs, betraying the calm he tried to project.

Galon leaned in until their noses nearly touched. "Listen carefully, boy. Your father's debt isn't satisfied until the mages say it is." He jabbed his finger toward Rasslow's face. "Now make everything right as rain. Tell me where to find her."

The smile he offered held no warmth, lips pressed tight, eyes dead as stones.

The clouds above parted. Moonlight flooded the camp, and in that sudden brightness, Rasslow caught a movement near the Northmen's encampment. A familiar silhouette darted between shadows Dagmar. His heart hammered against his ribs.

In the valley below, eighteen haphazardly pitched tents huddled around a towering mage's fire like frightened children around a stern parent. The flames cast long, erratic shadows that seemed to reach for the surrounding forest. Finrod, Blair, Dagmar, and Arbor belly-crawled through the underbrush, their bodies pressed against damp earth.

The crackling fire and occasional cries of pain from the imprisoned Northmen masked the soft rustle of their passage. Arbor's elvish eyes scanned the perimeter with practiced precision. Finrod mouthed a silent prayer, his lips barely moving. Blair's fingers hovered near his sword hilt, restrained only by Shandar's instruction to kill as a last resort.

They targeted the tent farthest from the mage's fire, where shadows gathered thickest. Dagmar would cut the ropes while the others stood ready. Each tent loomed in the darkness, ropes pulled taut like the strings of a trap ready to spring.

Dagmar reached the first tent, unsheathing a knife honed to wicked sharpness. The blade caught the firelight as he sliced through the first rope. The canvas sagged but remained upright exactly as planned. It would collapse later when they needed the distraction.

His heart keeping time with his quick, shallow breaths, Dagmar moved to the next tent. One down, seventeen to go. His hands worked with practiced efficiency, each cut precise and controlled.

Without warning, one tent collapsed completely. The others took this as their signal and began cutting faster, no longer trying to keep the structures upright. Voices called out to those inside: surrender or die.

A mage spotted Dagmar, his hand erupting in flame. Dagmar froze mid-stride as a fireball hurtled past him, striking a tent that burst into flames. Their cover blown, Dagmar abandoned stealth for speed, racing along the row of tents, slashing ropes as he went.

From the hillside above, Shandar's answering fireballs streaked toward the mages, exploding against invisible barriers but drawing their attention away from the ground assault.

Galon's head snapped toward the commotion. Rasslow saw his opportunity.

"I believe she is here!" he shouted, leaping backward. In one fluid motion, he drew his sword and drove it deep into Galon's neck. Blood spurted in a hot arc as the mage's eyes widened in shock.

Moirae shrieked, a sound like metal scraping stone. She lunged, fastening needle-sharp teeth into Rasslow's forearm. Pain lanced up to his shoulder. He reversed his grip and smashed the sword's pommel against her skull. The impact knocked her free, sending her small body tumbling beneath the wagon where she lay motionless.

Wincing, Rasslow tore a strip from Galon's sleeve and bound it tightly around the bite. Blood seeped through the makeshift bandage as he turned and sprinted toward the knoll where his companions fought.

He was ten paces from the nearest tent when an invisible wall stopped him cold. His face rebounded as though he'd struck stone, his knees buckling on impact. He landed hard; the breath knocked from his lungs. His sword clattered beside him.

Through watering eyes, he looked toward the warrior mages' fire. A man stood there unlike any Rasslow had seen before, wild hair and a full black beard interwoven with glass beads that glinted in the firelight. A tattoo of black lightning forked across his face, dividing cold gray eyes.

The mage raised his hands. Darkness gathered between his palms, then shot toward Rasslow a bolt of pure shadow. Rasslow raised his arms instinctively, but indecision paralyzed him. Jump left? Roll right? Run? His mind raced with possibilities while his body remained frozen.

He waited for death, hoping it would be quick.

The black energy was a pace away when it shattered like glass, fragments spraying harmlessly around him. Rasslow whipped around to see what had happened.

On the hill behind him, clouds rolled across the moon, plunging the scene into darkness. But through the gloom, he could make out a soft red glow of Shandar, turning away.

Shandar and Salem crouched at the edge of the small hill overlooking the mages' camp. The mages' fire burned atop a rocky outcropping, casting an orange glow across the valley where the tents stood in irregular rows. They kept low, hidden in the shadows cast by scrubby bushes.

Shandar's heart thundered against her ribs as she peered over the ridge. The scene below made her blood freeze. Rasslow stood facing a tall, skeletal man and a diminutive creature she recognized immediately. Her breath caught in her throat. She knew that man. Galon Valdove. The wagon behind them sent a spike of pain through her temple, memories threatening to surface. She opened her mouth but couldn't speak.

One tent below collapsed Dagmar's signal. The rescue had begun.

Drawing a deep breath, Shandar rose to her full height. Heat gathered in her palms as she hurled two fireballs toward the mages' fire. They struck with explosive force, scattering embers and creating instant chaos.

Movement caught her eye as Rasslow driving his sword into Galon's neck, the small creature attacking him, then being thrown aside. Rasslow ran toward a tent but crashed into an invisible barrier, falling backward.

One mage turned, his tattooed face contorting with rage. Black energy gathered around his hands, then shot toward Rasslow. Shandar's chest tightened with fear, but instinct took over. She focused her will, channeling her power not into fire, but into protection.

The black wave struck her invisible shield and exploded into fragments.

Salem gripped her arm, pulling her back from the edge. "Down!" he hissed. "They've seen you!"

Crouching behind a tree, Rasslow assessed the battlefield. Two mages now watched the hill where Shandar stood. The other two faced the tents below, where Dagmar, Arbor, and Finrod engaged with the Northmen. Fireballs launched toward the mages dissipated harmlessly against their invisible barriers.

Glancing up, Rasslow saw Salem whisper something to Shandar. She shook her head, eyes fixed forward. The sight of those two together sent a chill through him. Their combined power was something even the mages might fear.

Screams erupted from the mages' fire. Rasslow turned in time to see the ground beneath the mages and their fire simply vanish. They plummeted into the sudden pit, landing hard amidst tumbling logs and flaming debris. Before they could recover, Shandar restored the earth above them, sealing them in their makeshift tomb.

Silence fell over the camp like a heavy blanket. The magical barriers surrounding the tents faded like morning mist. Dazed prisoners appeared, blinking in the moonlight as though waking from a nightmare.

At the base of the hill, the companions reunited. Embraces and forearm clasps were exchanged, relief clear in every face. Before anyone could address the betrayal hanging unspoken between them, Dagmar stepped forward.

"We suffered no serious injuries," he reported, his golden eyes narrowed in concentration. "Four Northmen refused to surrender and were lost. Fourteen remain disarmed and awaiting judgment." He nodded toward Shandar. "We followed your instructions to avoid killing when possible, Mistress. What shall we do with the prisoners?"

Shandar's shoulders slumped slightly. "Send them home," she said, color rising in her cheeks. "Let them take their possessions, the wagon too. They've suffered enough."

Rika slipped behind Shandar, whispering in her ear. Both women turned to look at Rasslow.

The moment had come. Rasslow stepped forward, arms crossed over his chest. "It was me," he admitted, his voice steady despite his shuffling feet. "I gave up our position. They threatened my father because of his debts. Since childhood, I was taught family comes first protect the family at all costs. I never imagined it would lead to this." He couldn't meet their eyes, his gaze fixed on the ground between them.

The others looked away, uncomfortable with his confession. Only Shandar approached him, her expression unreadable.

"And how do you feel now?" she asked quietly. "What family will you protect going forward?" She stepped back, giving him space to answer.

Rasslow squared his shoulders and met her gaze. "I was raised to protect my blood kin above all else. But the Ceremony of Making marks when we choose who we become." His voice grew stronger. "I choose to redefine family as those who care for me and those I care for in return. Give me the chance to prove myself, and I won't disappoint you again."

"What will you do to accomplish this?" Shandar asked, her forehead creased with doubt.

Rasslow planted his feet firmly, standing tall. "I'll make it right as rain."

Shandar's eyes shot open, a torrent of horror, agony, and terror flooding through them like a raging storm. Her gaze locked onto his, and she erupted with an otherworldly glow. Black. Rasslow was engulfed in flames, but never realized as the inferno devoured him, leaving nothing but oblivion in its wake. The air crackled with heat and the acrid stench of burning flesh filled his nostrils. A searing pain, intense and all-consuming, blossomed where he stood, quickly replaced by a cold, infinite nothingness. The last thing he saw was Shandar's glowing eyes, the last thing he felt was unimaginable pain, the last thing he heard was the roar of the unnatural fire.

Maroon and gold banners snapped in the wind above Newberg's gates, declaring in bold letters: **"THE HORDE OF DESTRUCTION IS A LIE"** and **"KEEP MONDE MARVELOUS."** Queen Ellis Whyte-Willow's jaw clenched at the sight. She felt a surge of anger, but also something darker: unease. How could they shrug off danger so casually when every soul fleeing toward these walls carried desperation in their eyes?

Newberg's ramparts rose as tall as three men piled one atop another, circling a grid of neat, three-story buildings. Only two exits punctured the walls: the main gate on King's Road and a smaller passage to the docks. South of town, engineers had long ago carved an artificial river for barges to unload, now the linchpin of her evacuation plan.

Ellis's heart pounded as she took in the bottleneck at the gate. Families, wounded men, children clutched too-small bundles of possessions. Officials huddled together, exchanging heated whispers instead of smoothing the flow. She swallowed, torn between fury at their incompetence and guilt that she'd entrusted them with this moment.

"Sho is with Var...or so she'd been told. Good. But what if it wasn't enough? She could be queen a while, she reminded herself. She had to be.

She motioned for her wagon to roll forward. Stepping down, she squared her shoulders and strode to the nearest cluster of administrators. A tremor of doubt ran through her, was she imposing, or offering needed help?

"Excuse me," she said, voice firm though her stomach fluttered. "May I have a moment?"

One elderly man in a fine coat and strange half-boots looked up, scowl in place. Recognition flickered in his eyes, and he mouthed a silent greeting. Ellis exhaled, forcing steadiness.

"We need order," she told them, suppressing the tremor in her tone. "Land-bound refugees turn right, follow King's Road out to the camp. Sea-bound keep left through the gate, head to the river barges for onward passage. Post one guide on each side of the divide. No exceptions."

The old man blinked, then smiled as if pride had replaced confusion. "That's, exactly, what I said," he stammered, smoothing his coat. "The Queen's orders are clear! Mable, Sorren, you handle the right. Star and I take the left. Let's move!"

They dispersed with brisk purpose, and for a moment Ellis felt relief. Then she caught the old man's low whisper to his aide: "She's really going to be furious when she reaches the river."

Her chest tightened. Furious? No one understood what lay ahead, what horrors might greet them on the water's edge. Ellis took a steadying breath. Was she ready to face it herself?

A hundred yards away from where Rasslow had stood, Shandar collapsed. Her legs buckled as if the strings holding her upright had been severed. She crumpled to the earth, arms wrapped around herself, trembling like a leaf in autumn's final storm.

Rika was beside her in an instant. "Breathe," she whispered, encircling Shandar with steady arms. "Just breathe."

Shandar's eyes remained fixed on the smoking patch of ground where Rasslow had stood moments before. Where her fire had consumed him when he'd spoken those five words: "I'll make it right as rain."

The same words her mother's debtor had whispered, all those years ago.

A violent shiver shook Shandar, and she clutched Rika tighter, tears carving tracks through smoke and soot. "Will you merge with me? Please... I need you." Her voice cracked like fragile glass.

Circling them, the others formed a living barrier of turned backs. Finrod advanced on the prisoners, Kumar and Arbor patrolled the perimeter, Dagmar shadowed Finrod's steps, Salem drifted near Baltan, and Blair hovered two paces back, close enough to defend, far enough to grant privacy.

I'm here, sister. Rika projected into Shandar's mind. The world fell away. Rika found herself in a long stone corridor stretching into darkness. Countless wooden doors lined the walls, each sealed tight except for one. That door stood slightly ajar, pulsing with sickly light. From beyond it came the high, thin scream of a child, the creak of wagon wheels, the sound of a girl begging.

Without pause, Rika shoved the door shut.

"Lock it," Shandar's voice echoed around her. "Something only you would recognize."

Rika pressed her palm against the wood. A silver moonstone materialized in the door's center, its surface swirling with the same astral light as her magic. The corridor seemed to exhale.

"Your mother taught you this?" Rika asked, her mental voice stripped of all courtly disguise.

"She did." Shandar's presence in the corridor felt smaller somehow, diminished. "After she traded me to clear her debts. She taught me to lock away the memories so I could function. So I wouldn't scream when she needed me quiet."

Rika's vision blurred. "Shandar…"

"Now you know what I am." A bitter laugh echoed through the mental space. "Damaged goods."

"I'll be right back," Rika promised, withdrawing gently from Shandar's mind.

She returned to her body with a gasp. Shandar sat motionless beside her, eyes vacant. Rika rose unsteadily and caught Salem's gaze. With a slight gesture, she drew the fairy creature aside.

"Her mother," Rika whispered, shaking. "She built walls in Shandar's mind to hide what she'd done to her own daughter."

Salem's wings stilled, a rare sign of her complete attention. "And?"

"I saw it. Her mother gave her to a man to settle a debt." Rika's voice cracked. "Shandar was eleven."

Salem's pale face hardened. "Lashnar didn't choose her for her strength," she said. "The temple poured power into her to bury those horrors, not to free her from them."

"What do I do?" Rika asked. "Rasslow's words tore everything open."

Salem's eyes, ancient and knowing, met Rika's. "Tell her she had no choice. That Rasslow's death was necessary, inevitable." Her voice dropped lower. "She needs that certainty more than she needs truth."

Before Rika could respond, a sound cut through the clearing, raw and primal.

The sound that tore from Blair's throat wasn't a scream, it was something deeper, more fundamental. The sound of something inside him breaking beyond repair.

He sank to his knees, doubled over as if physically struck. In his hands, clutched so tightly his knuckles whitened, was a simple golden circlet.

The king's crown.

Shandar moved before anyone else could react. The vacancy in her eyes vanished as she lunged forward, catching Blair before he collapsed completely. She pulled him against her, one hand cradling his head as his body convulsed with silent sobs.

"I've got you," she murmured, rocking him gently. Her eyes found Rika's over Blair's shoulder, wide with realization as she stared at the crown in Blair's white-knuckled grip.

"Lashnar preserve us," Shandar whispered. "Blair is king."

The company froze in the fading light, suspended between one world and the next, between the quest that had driven them and the kingdom that now called its ruler home.

END